MIKE RICKSECKER'S

GHOSTORIAN CASE FILES

VOLUME 1

If you are reading this line of text then you understand the spirit of my writing. Keep searching.

First Edition:
First printing

Front cover photo:
The Ghostorian by Arielle Ricksecker

Back cover artwork:
Eerie House by Collin Ricksecker

PUBLISHED BY HAUNTED ROAD MEDIA, LLC
www.hauntedroadmedia.com

United States of America

To Collin, Arielle, Chase, and Cameron

ACKNOWLEDGMENTS

This work is more than just two years in the making, as I drifted back into investigations prior to Society of the Haunted's 2011 inception, including remnants of my childhood within *The Dream Journal*. These things would not have been possible over the years without the help and/or support of the following individuals:

The Oklahoma Historical Society, *The Oklahoman*, Society of the Haunted, Vanessa Hogle, Cathy Nance, Chris Borthick, Johnny Longan, Logan Corelli, Christy Clark, Kelly Johnston, Robbie Thomas, Margaret Ehrlich, Rob Gutro, Andrea Perron.

The entire Ricksecker clan, including Mom and Dad, Toni Yarosh, and Collin, Arielle, Chase, and Cameron Ricksecker.

TABLE OF CONTENTS

INTRODUCTION

When I'm on a paranormal investigation one of the things I always make sure to have with me is a notepad. I believe it's one of the most under-utilized tools in the field today, but it is extremely useful in keeping track of what the property owner has told you about a location in interviews and tours of the locations. Far too many times am I on an investigation and someone asks me, "Now, what was it that happened in this room again?"

Usually, my memory serves me well, but if I don't recall I at least have my notepad handy. If I didn't have it with me then that investigator would be out of luck. It's bad enough having investigators forget within hours the historic events that happened in a particular room. What about days after the investigation when they're trying to piece back together what happened and they can't recall any of the pertinent facts? What if an investigator captures a fantastic EVP but fails to relate it to any information of the location simply because he or she hadn't written it down?.

My notes are transcribed and then kept in virtual folders on my computer for reference as we go through the case and for any future projects. Some of these notes on historic locations have become instrumental in piecing together the shows I've filmed for YouTube. Other notes were essential in uncovering the tragic history of the house in Edmond, Oklahoma, that was featured on *The Haunted*.

What the *Ghostorian Case Files* aims to do is to give you a taste of what it would be like to crack open my file cabinet, pull out a folder on any particular case, and start reading through the notes I've taken. In order to protect the innocent (and, sometimes, guilty), the cases in these stories are fictional, but they are based on real history and legends from throughout the world.

For instance, the inscription of King Naram Sin of Chaldea is real, the histories behind the Black Bear Church and Blue Belle Saloon locations are true, and Dr. Walter Freeman did commit his terrible acts.

Giving the mixture of truth and fiction and the style in which I've written these tales, I've been calling the *Ghostorian Case Files* hybrid paranormal research written works, and it's fitting enough. One may even call this type of work experimental, and I've received a mix of criticism, both good and bad, on the way it's written.

My dear reader, that just happens to be the style of the work. Just keep in mind that you are holding open a folder of case notes from one of my investigations and not a book. It may look and feel like a book, but that is not how it reads.

The first three case files in this volume were previously published on Kindle as standalones, and "The Inscription Of Evil Times" also made an appearance in *Campfire Tales: Midwest*. "The Dream Journal" is new and is something I truly keep because of the number of dreams I've really had that have come to pass. All of the Exhibits in "The Dream Journal" are actually true.

INTRODUCTION

For years now I have been defining the term "Ghostorian" as:

One who researches and investigates a ghost and the place in which it haunts.

I, Mike Ricksecker, am a Ghostorian.

This case came to me out of nowhere. A man who called himself Dr. Patrick approached me one fine afternoon and asked me if I would consider researching for him a matter of grave importance. I asked him what he had in mind and he proceeded to unveil documents concerning an ancient tablet with an archaic inscription and an old tattered journal he claimed dated to the 1860s in Iowa.

Dr. Patrick insisted the two historic pieces were related and it is from those two sources that this investigation began. I did not expect at all for it to take me where it did.

I have opened my case file to present these thirteen exhibits. Make of it what you will.

EXHIBIT 1
JOURNAL ENTRY #1

It began in darkness. Elle awoke coughing and then took to the fever. Within just days she was taken from us and we are still in complete shock. We can only assume that the Lord had bigger plans for her, but the children are now without their mother and me without a wife. Life suddenly became much more difficult than it already was and I am without desire.

The service was today. Elle's family attended and Reverend Williams presided. I can't say it wasn't a lovely service but it was preceded with a small mystery. Yesterday, as we took to the task of digging the plot near the cottonwood we unearthed a stone tablet of sorts. Upon it was carved an inscription unlike any we had ever seen. We removed it from the ground and brought it up to the house so we could continue our labor.

I asked Reverend Williams about the inscription today after the service and showed him the tablet, and he claimed to not know what it meant. Yet it struck me that he may not have been entirely truthful and somewhere in his words was a falsehood. I know I ought not to say that about the Lord's trusted servant, but I believe Reverend Williams does know something of the tablet and its inscription. Why he wouldn't tell me I cannot guess.

I may ask Elle's sister to stay with us a spell. She's a spinster, but a temporary caretaker for the younger children may lend to be helpful.

Dr. Patrick's Note:

While this is not the first encounter with the tablet and the inscription in the chronology, I have presented it first to illustrate the innocent nature in which it seemed acquired. It is also quite suspect that they buried their loved one in the same hole from whence it came.

EXHIBIT 2
THE INSCRIPTION

<u>Dr. Patrick's Note</u>:

This is not the first I have seen of this inscription. My original observance was in Istanbul on a tablet in a museum. My published notes on the matter are as follows:

In the museum at Constantinople the writer saw an inscription upon an old stone. It was by King Naram Sin of Chaldea, 3800 years B.C., and it said,

We have fallen upon evil times
and the world has waxed very old and wicked.
Politics are very corrupt.
Children are no longer respectful to their parents.

This old and ever-recurring complaint does not depend upon any actual deterioration of the times, for the times are constantly growing better. It comes usually from older people whose outlook may be biased by subjective conditions due to decaying powers and by the tendency to regard all changes as changes for the worse, the only really good times being the bright days of our own youth.

It is curious that a facsimile of the inscription was found here in America thousands of years after the original was carved. Its provenance is important but indiscernible at this time. This is a matter more appropriate for my colleagues in archeology, but I am drawn to the mystery of this tale and why it has found me again.

EXHIBIT 3A
JOURNAL ENTRY #2

Elle's sister has been murdered, stabbed six times with one of the kitchen knives. Reverend Williams called upon the house and offered his blessing. He has called us to prayer to repent for we have lost the way of the Lord during these dark times. Sin has plagued the home since Elle caught the fever. We've been cursed for our sins. I should never have lied to Rogers about what happened to his horse during that hail storm.

The children are frightened. Young **Mary** even claimed to the Reverend that she had seen her mother just a fortnight ago walking the grounds in the moonlight. Blasphemous child, according to Reverend Williams. My family is falling apart.

The mayor is interested in the stone tablet that was found at Elle's gravesite. He believes if the interest in the railroad doesn't hold fast then maybe scholars would be interested in local history. I can't imagine a scholar being interested in this land at all.

Dr. Patrick's Note:

This is the final entry on the final page of the journal. At this time it is unknown whether there is another volume with additional entries concerning the family in question.

EXHIBIT 3B
GHOSTORIAN'S NOTES

It is possible that the journal may have been written by Elijah Dobson. He was born in 1833 in Lancaster, Pennsylvania, and married Giselle Pruitt in 1855. Giselle died in 1867 in Conover, Iowa. She was survived by her husband, sons William and Paul, and daughters Martha, Elizabeth, and Mary. She had a sister, Elvira, who died in 1868, also in Conover, Iowa.

Elijah Dobson died in 1881 in Kansas City, Missouri. Census records from 1870 show that the family moved there prior to the 1870 record. Oddly, Mary was not listed on the census record and I can find no record of her death.

Although not unusual for records of that period of time, I can find no cause of death for Giselle, Elvira, or Elijah. The remaining children, save for Elizabeth, scattered across the country. William passed away in Grantsville, Utah, in 1922, Paul in Villisca, Iowa, in 1913, and Martha as Martha Johnston in Guthrie, Oklahoma, in 1931. Elizabeth never married and passed away in Kansas City in 1943. Although I can find no original record of purchase, the house Elizabeth **lived** in when she died was still in the name of her father, Elijah, upon her death.

Understandably, there is some room for doubt, these are those closest records I could find to match the journal entries with that timeframe in Iowa. Giselle can easily be shortened to Elle, she had a sister who died just a year later, she had a daughter by the name of Mary who was considered young, and there are other children in the picture.

I will continue to look for additional information to support my theory that this is the family in question.

EXHIBIT 4
AN IOWA GHOST ENCOUNTER

Ghostorian's Note:

The following was submitted by inquiry via internet in a request for local folklore near former Conover, Iowa, after discovering a few reports of sightings near Calmar. These consisted of little one-liners such as:

"Along the trail outside of Calmar is an old foundation where an eerie mist forms on nights of the full moon."

"There's the foundation of an old witch's house near Calmar that is haunted by a freezing white mist on some nights even though it's warm outside."

From ghostmommy1985:

Although it's about 45 minutes away, we had all heard about the haunting along the Prairie Farmer Recreation Trail near Calmer and we wanted to make the trip to check it out. The legend as we've heard it is that if you sit in the center of the foundation of an old farm out near one of the fields then the temperature will drop about thirty degrees and a white mist will form around the foundation. Moans cry out from the mist and if you're not careful then hands will pull at you and drag you into a pit of hell in the middle of the ruins.

Well, that's not exactly how we experienced it, but we did experience *something*.

We got the location of the foundation from a reluctant local, but we had to explain ourselves pretty thoroughly and Casey bought him a case of beer. Apparently, a lot of teens head out there to party and make out, but we told him we were more interested in finding the remains of the structure and maybe discovering something historical. When he told us of all the partying out there, we suddenly weren't very hopeful to find much of anything.

Fortunately, we did find what seemed to be an old stone foundation and, just like we'd been told, it was littered **with** empty beer cans and cold embers from little fires. The three of us hung out for a while taking pictures and just getting a sense of the place, but there really wasn't much. We kicked around the embers and the beer cans, but there were far too many to pick out, and we looked at the stonework of the foundation, which was weather beaten and littered with graffiti. I thought it was a bust.

My boyfriend, Chuck, noticed a gnarly old tree about a hundred feet away from the foundation and insisted we go check it out. There weren't any leaves on it and it seemed like it had been dead for years, but there it stood. It was much colder by the tree than it had been at the foundation. Again, we took all kinds of pictures, but as we continued to stay a mist began forming around us and the tree.

As the mist grew thicker the tree seemed to take on its own gray glow. It got so cold that we started seeing our breath. That's when the woman appeared. She didn't make any sound, but she walked into the mist wretching and convulsing as if she were sick. We stepped away from her, but she looked up at me and all she had for eyes were these deep, dark pits.

We ran out of there as fast as we could.

EXHIBIT 5
DOCTOR'S NOTES

It must be noted that the full inscription from the stone in Istanbul has two additional lines:

Each man wants to make himself conspicuous and write a book.
The end of the world is manifestly drawing nigh.

Admittedly, I did not include these in my previously published piece since the bit about book writing seemed extraneous while the end of the world comment is borderline ridiculous. It merely propounds a psychology of elders that the youth of whom they do not relate must be bringing about the end of the world with their changes.

What is interesting to note about these two lines on this particular tablet presented to me is that they're nearly scratched off. It is likely that these scratchings occurred more recently than the original inscription and are not a correction on the part of the author, but I am no forensic expert on the matter.

I am still contemplating the possible purpose for vandalizing these two lines of the inscription and the mindset of one who would do so.

EXHIBIT 6
THE CONOVER FIRE

Conover, Iowa, no longer exists and is classified as a ghost town. Originally intended to be a railway hub, at one point boasting about 200 buildings, including 32 saloons, in 1865, Conover's sparse remnants are now scattered along the outskirts of Calmar.

There was only ever one mayor of Conover, Captain V.C. Jacobs, elected in 1867. The election was controversial, however, as expenses for it exceeded the funds in the town's treasury and **the** new clerk, J.J. Haug, proceeded to do nothing to repay the debt. Compounding the dire money situation was the continued growth of the railroad to the north and west and the development of Calmar as the eastern terminus and junction.

The town began to dwindle, but the final devastation of Conover came with a great fire that destroyed numerous buildings, including the one serving as the small city hall and courthouse. Scores of important records and documents were destroyed making the town's history and its financial perils difficult to research. It is noted that town councilmen included Colonel G.D. Pagent, Charles Syndan, and Captain George Q. Gardener, but there is no way to know if they played any significant role in the town's development and demise. The devastation of the fire caused most of the inhabitants to pack up their belongings and buildings and move to Calmar.

There are no records about what caused the fire, just a few notes that it occurred.

EXHIBIT 7
THE ORIGINAL INSCRIPTION?

<u>Dr. Patrick's Notes</u>:

While further delving into the provenance of the tablet I happened across a dusty text which spoke of a similar inscription but much more lengthy in scope. This inscription predates the Chaldean one from 3800 B.C. and more likely reigns from Egypt much closer to 5000 B.C. As is usually the case, older texts are influences for more recent ones; the youth, while separating themselves from their elders, still retaining some of the previous generation's history and wisdom while devising their own.

Whoever has ears let them hear,
These are the words of the first and last.
Your afflictions and poverty are known,
All are cast upon a bed of suffering.
Evil times have befallen us,
The world has waxed very old and wicked.
Corruption riddles our kings,
Children usurp their parents.
Every man thinks himself a scribe,
The end of the world is manifestly drawing nigh.
The dead shall walk and shall speak,

Bodies shall be brought forth to the Aged One.
Mothers shall beat their breasts and weep,
All come to the Great House for purification.
Worms feed upon the bodies of men and drink their blood,
Hearts pass through fire and darkness.
Drops of blood shall bring forth the soul,
Storms in the sky burn red.

EXHIBIT 8
GHOSTORIAN'S JOURNAL

This is an excerpt from my personal case journal...

<u>Day 21</u>:

The challenges in this case are many. There is nobody to interview since the events that transpired around the stone tablet's discovery happened almost 150 years ago. Most of the records from that time were destroyed in a fire. The journal entry that I believe to be the writing of Elijah Dobson was given to me by Dr. Patrick. I find myself cobbling together what few facts remain with the dissection of the local folklore.

One of my jobs as a Ghostorian has been to research and discover the original truth of a tale that has spun into a myth. These stories originated from somewhere either to explain something that couldn't be explained at the time or it was a story that morphed out of control in the retelling. With virtually no records available I am finding it essential to decipher these tales.

A convulsing apparition could correlate to the journal tale of the sickly Elle Dobson, but as far as I can tell that wasn't a part of the local folklore. That was a new report from the woman that answered the inquiry. The local folklore has centered around the foundation and the mist. Yet, that group of people left the foundation to observe an old tree around which the mist formed.

Elijah Dobson spoke of a cottonwood tree in his journal, but cottonwoods only survive about 70 years. At the very most, if the trees are related at all, the current tree could be a seed from the one near the burial site of Elle Dobson and where the tablet was unearthed.

Day 24:

I've been running the few names I have of locals to Conover through the meat grinder of searches to see if I get any hits, but most have proved unfruitful. I found a quick reference to J.J. Haug, a Swiss immigrant, who settled in Marysville, which was later named Calmar after learning there was another town in Iowa named Marysville.

While I didn't find a direct reference to Captain V.C. Jacobs, the mayor of Conover, I did find an 1880 reference to a V. Jacobs at nearby Fort Atkinson as someone holding interest in the old fort's structures, although he was not part of the 1880 census there.

Day 26:

I'm not even sure what to make of this. When I awoke today I discovered all of the original material that I had received from Dr. Patrick in a heap of ashes on my desk. Nothing else was touched or burned, but everything from him was destroyed. Fortunately, I had made copies and my records are intact, but the fact that just one pile of material when up in smoke – and the smoke alarm did not go off – is absolutely bizarre. There is nothing to salvage, but I am storing the ash in a plastic container for who knows what future purpose.

Day 31:

My searching has not been in vain after all. I was placed in contact today with a woman who claims to be a decedent of Charles Syndan who briefly served on the council of Conover. She was reluctant to talk much at all about her great-grandfather, but she thought it important that I listen to the brief tales she had been told of his time in Conover.

The record of her tale from our phone conversation:

"Grandpa Charles was a private man, but he had a few tales he would spin. Some, I'm sure, were great yarns, and every once in a while he would talk about this little town that no longer exists known as Conover. He only spent a short spell there serving as a councilman, but that time was enough for him.

The town was broke and the promises from the railroad had been broken. Conover was going to go belly up, which was of great dismay to the mayor who was newly elected and was quite enjoying his little reign of power, small as it was. He was frantic in trying to figure out how to bring money back into the town to keep the business there. Most of it was in saloons from the connections to the railroad that was leaving, so Grandpa Charles wasn't confident anything could seriously be done.

Well, suddenly, the mayor called a meeting of the council to talk to them about a story he'd heard from the **Reverend** about some ancient artifact that one of the locals had dug up. He thought if there was history buried out in the cow pastures of Conover then the town could attract the business of a different sort in the scholars and intellectuals of the day. He was laughed right out of the meeting house.

Now, Grandpa Charles, while he didn't believe any sort of migration of scholars to Conover was even probable let alone could save the town, he was interested in this story he'd heard about an ancient relic. What exactly was it and where did it come from? He found the mayor and the

Reverend in a heated argument in a back room of one of the saloons carrying on about who should have ownership of this artifact. The Reverend insisted such things belonged in the hands of the church while the mayor argued that it was an object of history and science, not to be **trapped** by the Church, and they should use it and anything else they unearthed to found a university.

"I'd rather see this town burn in hell!" Grandpa Charles overheard the Reverend yell.

Now, the very next day the town did burn down, or, at least, most of it. Grandpa Charles was sure the Reverend had held true to his word, but to Grandpa's dismay when the mayor addressed the town after the fire he claimed children had accidentally started a fire behind one of the saloons.

Nobody questioned the matter and Conover was soon abandoned, but Grandpa Charles always believed the Reverend was the one that set the blaze. As for the ancient artifact that was supposed to have been discovered on the land, well, my great-grandfather never did learn exactly what that was or where it ended up. Most people moved to Calmar and lived out the rest of their days in peace while others moved on their own separate ways completely."

EXHIBIT 9
THE FORMICARIUS

<u>Dr. Patrick's Notes</u>:
From the identical source as I had received the stone tablet I have received into my possession another peculiar object: a translated copy of *The Formicarius* of Johannes Nider. The text is quite unfamiliar to me and dates to the 1420s. I was instructed to note the following passages:

"There are, or there very recently were (as both the same inquisitor and Lord Peter have told me, and as is well known among the public) in the territory of Bern, a great many witches of both sexes who greatly hated human nature and assumed the likenesses of various kinds of beasts, especially those kinds that devour children.

In the town of Boltingen in the diocese of Lausanne there lived a man named Stadelin, a great witch, who was arrested by the same Lord Peter, the judge of the district. Stadelin had entered a house where a man and wife lived and by his witchcraft killed seven successive infants in her womb."

"**After** this fashion was I seduced; and my wife also, whom I believe of so great pertinacity that she will endure the flames rather than confess the least whit of truth, but alas, we are both guilty. What the young man was seen to die in great contrition. His wife, however, though convicted by the testimony of witnesses, would not confess the truth even under the torture or in death; but, when the fire was prepared for her by the executioner, she uttered in most evil words a curse upon him, and was so burned."

"Finally, this year I learned from the aforesaid inquisitor that in the duchy of Lausanne certain witches cooked their own newly born babies, and ate them. Moreover, the means of learning such art was, so he said, that the witches came together in a certain convocation, and through their efforts, they saw a demon visibly in an assumed human form, to whom the disciple had to pledge that he would deny Christianity, would never adore the Eucharist, and would secretly trample on the cross whenever he could."

"These two knew how to carry over a third part of the dung, hay, or grain, or whatever sort of things, when it pleased them, from their neighbor's field to their own field, with no on seeing them, how to raise enormous hailstorms and destructive winds with lightning, how to hurl children walking near water, in the sight of their parents, into that with no one seeing them, how to bring sterility in people and animals, how to harm those near them both bodily and in goods."

EXHIBIT 10
GHOSTORIAN'S NOTES ON THE FORMICARIUS

Pre-Note:

Before I get into my notes on *The Formicarius*, I think it would be wise to note that just before Dr. Patrick presented me with the text I spotted a little girl spying on me through the window of my office. She was in an old weather-beaten dress and she looked rather sad. I ran outside to talk to her, but she was gone by the time I got to where she had been standing by the window. Now, thinking back on the girl, the dress she was wearing was extremely outdated.

The Formicarius is a precursor to the *Malleus Maleficarum* (The Witch's Hammer) and is said to have heavily influenced it. Aside from two minor points, why it has suddenly been thrust into the mix of this mystery is beyond me.

The tales of witchcraft in Nider's *Formicarius* are largely focused in areas of Switzerland. A number of the inhabitants of the area around Conover were Swiss immigrants. Perhaps they brought this old tome with them.

There's also the little one-liner ghost sighting from the area:

"There's the foundation of an old witch's house near Calmar that is haunted by a freezing white mist on some nights even though it's warm outside."

At first I figured the description of a witch's house was conjecture on the part of the teller, or mythology added into the mix over the years of the reported mist. When people tell tales of seeing things they like to add in their own explanations for the occurrence, which after many re-tellings over time suddenly become a pseudo fact of the event. This could still be the case, but perhaps a deeper reason why that is the case is because the culture of the people that lived there included stories of witches. Granted, we're talking a time period about 450 years after *The Formicarius* was written, but some cultural traits stick around for a long time. After all, my own Swiss ancestors fled to America in the late 1600s due to religious persecution, already more than 150 years from its authorship.

I also find it interesting in my brief research of Johannes Nider, some of the more extensive materials covering the subject were books coming out of Iowa State University.

EXHIBIT 11
GHOSTORIAN'S JOURNAL

<u>Day 36</u>:

Doctor Patrick has disappeared. I had been unable to contact him the past couple days which led me to seek him out at the hotel he'd been staying at. There was no answer at the door, so I asked the clerk at the service desk if the doctor had left. The clerk gave me a perplexed look and told me that he had never heard of Dr. Patrick and nobody had rented that room in weeks since it had been sealed off for renovation.

I went home puzzled and unsure what to do. I had assembled this web of history and tales that didn't make a whole lot of sense, and **the** one that had requested my help with it had vanished as if he'd never existed. I was dumbfounded even more when I returned home and found *The Formicarius* text I'd received from Dr. Patrick in a heap of ashes on my desk. Again, nothing else had been damaged.

EXHIBIT 12
THE LOST JOURNAL

<u>Ghostorian's Note</u>:
A small leather-bound journal showed up in my mail with no return address. It had only one entry.

Perhaps I should have just stolen the tablet from Dobson. Now who knows where it is. It's gone, and maybe it's no longer a part of this physical earthly plane. It would have been a prize in the hands of anyone with a bit of sense instead of that bumbling fool and his family. Instead, it got a hold of that little girl.

Children started a **fire** behind a saloon, indeed. It was one child, the youngest one, in fact, but it may not really have been her. I think I saw the devil in her eyes. The flames behind her rose in a motley sea of colors, and it spread from building to building like wildfire. I thought the world was ending as the skies stormed red. She calmly stalked the road through the middle of town, holding that great weight of a tablet. I have no idea how she managed it.

Of few that saw her other than I, some screamed "witch" while others screamed "demon," and each that did perished. I believe my silence saved me from her wrath while all others fled. Throughout the terror I stood still and silent and watched as she stoically walked straight out of Conover.

It was such a striking difference from the meek little girl that I observed in the window of her home, another time I stood silent and watched. I had stopped by the farm seeking a small contribution, and Elle was there only with the little one. Elijah was out working his field and the other children must have been off at school, but Rogers was there. I don't know what he shoved down the throat of that woman, but he made sure to tell her, "I know your husband lied about my horse, now he's not going to have his own horse no more!"

I didn't realize until Elle died that he was insulting her at the same time by calling her a horse. I thought he was just taking a hand to her and Elijah would see and deal with it. I expected one of Elijah's horses to show up dead, but no. I suppose it was one of many things I didn't understand throughout this entire tragedy. I didn't understand and I didn't act. I just stood silent and still and I didn't tell Dobson what Rogers had done.

And for it, my town that had been my dream is now gone.

V.C. Jacobs

EXHIBIT 13
FINAL THOUGHTS

Day 42:

This case is as open as it is closed. There are a myriad of loose ends that I don't expect will be tied up anytime soon, and I'm not sure I want to devote the time it would take into doing that right now.

I still have heard nothing of the mysterious Dr. Patrick, where he went and, really, where he had even come from. Just as quickly as he had come into my life he vanished. However, who is not vanishing is the little girl.

I will see her on occasion peering through the window at me as I work in my office. I waved to her once and she ran. I've noticed after multiple times of seeing her now that her vintage mid-Nineteenth century dress is dotted with droplets of dried blood and singed around the edges as if it had suffered a little fire damage. I've since been calling her Mary.

I don't know what may have happened to her after the Conover fire and if there is any rest for her soul. Perhaps she is looking for the tablet and thinks that Dr. Patrick gave it to me, but he never did and I have no idea where it may be. Perhaps there is a connection between the tablet and her mother that she seeks since her mother's body replaced the resting place of the tablet.

Like I said, there are too many loose ends.

There is still a longing, however, to uncover the origins of the tablet and its inscription and why it, apparently, holds such power. I expect whatever secrets it holds are as potent now as they were then – it always seems to be evil times, after all.

Mike Ricksecker
Ghostorian

INTRODUCTION

For years now I have been defining the term "Ghostorian" as:

One who researches and investigates a ghost and the place in which it haunts.

I, Mike Ricksecker, am a Ghostorian.

The genesis of this case begins with the skeletal remains of an old, decrepit church off a dirt road in the Middle of Nowhere, Oklahoma. Following an investigation late one night with members of Society of the Haunted, one of the crew offered to show us these ruins and the cemetery directly across from it since he'd had so many experiences there when he'd been a younger investigator. Numerous returns back, a YouTube video, and a television show episode later the story continues.

I'd received two letters, the first in the form of an email, within weeks of each other, and they set me on the path of digging deeper into the history of a location in which history was sparse. I would soon learn that the real history was more interpersonal and spiritual in nature rather than the facts of figures of past events.

I never imagined the story would venture as far as it did. I've presented my findings here in this noted journal for you to make your own conclusions.

EXHIBIT 1
THE FIRST LETTER

Dear Mr. Ricksecker,

I saw your "Church of Darkness" episode on TV and then watched your *Ghosts and Legends of Oklahoma* video on YouTube about Black Bear Church ad thought I should take a few minutes to write to you. You see, I witnessed a couple of those occult ceremonies you thought may have happened there.

You're right in thinking that sort of stuff went on there after the church had closed. Like anything else left abandoned it becomes a hot spot for anyone up to mischief. As a teen I used to drink there with a bunch of friends. We'd all get hammered and have sex, and I guess we thought it was cool that we were doing it in an old church. Perhaps we were too oblivious to anything else that might have been going on there, but I don't recall seeing anything unusual at the church back then.

During the 90s I got involved for a short period of time with a group that was practicing some sort of black magic. They were called The Magus but I can't remember if they were a part of any established cult or religion or if they were doing things on their own.

The first time we were out there we mostly just sat in a circle with candles and meditated. Our meditation didn't seem harmful at all and they all seemed like a good group of people. I do remember at one moment thinking I saw a black mass moving around up by the roof, but it was gone as quickly as it had come. It was the second time that was frightening.

In your video you pointed out a stone slab in a back room that you thought may have been used for animal sacrifices. That's exactly what we used it for. We walked into the church chanting and holding candles except for the group's leader who was carrying a black cat. He paraded that cat through the church, up the stairs, and to the stone slab. He held up the cat, said a few words I don't remember, and then decapitated the creature with a deer knife. We were all ordered to take blood from the cat and smear it across our faces, then form a circle in the middle of the sanctuary.

One of the others built a small fire while we chanted, then our leader cast the dead cat into the fire. Thick black smoke rose up and almost choked us out. For some strange reason we could hear the cries of the cat coming out of the fire and suddenly the remnants of the broken windows blew open. The black smoke was seemingly sucked out through them and the fire went out. It was pitch black in the church for a brief moment then moonlight poured in through the windows. A chill ran up my spine when I saw that looking in at us through the windows from outside were these short, dark shadow people, almost half human, half shadow. Everything about them was dark and they had sunken eyes that were black as well. They didn't move. They just stood there staring in at us.

Suddenly, from the ceiling there was a growl, and we looked up. Some sort of black creature was crawling around up there with long, gangly arms and legs. I couldn't see its head and I didn't want to. I'd had enough at that point and ran out of the church. I looked back and saw that the building was surrounded by the short **shadow** people then turned and ran down the dirt road.

I wasn't but a few feet past the cemetery when I smacked into one of the locals. He must have been one of the ranch hands the way he was dressed, and he asked me what was wrong. I told him about the ceremony, and he tilted his hat and said, "So they finally went and done it. Get out of here and catch your train."

He walked past me and I kept running down the road. About an hour later I was walking along Route 64 when one of the cult members picked me up. He chewed me out for being a chicken shit and running off, but I told him this wasn't for me and I never went out with them again. I did ask if the ceremony got broken up by the locals and told him about the guy I ran into on the dirt road, but I guess he just let the cult finish their ceremony. I thought for sure he'd try to break it up or call the cops.

In any case, I hope my story is helpful to you somehow in your research of the location if you're still investigating it. I don't know what goes on there these days, but it's a place I'll definitely never go back to. It sounds like the creature I saw moving around the ceiling, the crawler as you've called it, is still there.

Sincerely,

"Jack"

EXHIBIT 2
THE SECOND LETTER

Dear Mr. Ricksecker,

I reckon you don't remember me, but we met once before in spirit. You and some others stood out in a cemetery late one night while a bunch of others was off over in the church across the road. I stood not far from the grave marked "Unknown Cowboy" while you all conversed with me and I told you of the dark presence that lurked yonder by the church. It's been ever since then that I have become concerned about our friend known as the unknown cowboy.

You see, in my travels he has made himself known to me. I suppose you could say he has latched on to me since that night as we spoke there near his earthly remains and talked of the church, the cemetery, and of him. I reckon he's wanting some sort of acknowledgment and peace about his – I guess you'd call it his departure from his earthly body. From the small talk we've had it seems like he's got some resentments and he's really a sad kind of man.

I was fixing to reach out to you before but now I finally have because I've heard that you've got a specialty in finding out about the history behind the spirits that live in certain places. I'm hoping you can figure out who this unknown cowboy really is so I can put him at ease while he tags along with me.

You can write me about your findings through the post if you'd be so kind as to look into this matter.

Yours eternally,

Bartholomew Jenkins

Ghostorian's Note:

While the request is odd enough, the identity of the requestor is even odder. Bartholomew Jenkins is dead.

EXHIBIT 3
CASE BACKGROUND NOTES

The "Unknown Cowboy" marker is located in Black Bear Cemetery in Olive Township, Oklahoma, just across the dirt road from what is known as "Black Bear Church," but when it was in operation was known as the New Bethany Baptist Church. The church ceased services sometime in the late 1960s or early 1970s, and has since fallen into severe disrepair. The cemetery is kept up by the locals who have family buried there. The identity of the unknown cowboy has remained a mystery for decades.

Black Bear, both the church and the cemetery, have been featured in *Ghost and Legends of Oklahoma*, *Campfire Tales: Midwest*, and on the television show *My Ghost Story* in which I was also featured. I have also produced a YouTube documentary on the location here:
https://youtu.be/SJTOo-k3E3c

There is sparse information about the history of the location. The cemetery was once known as the Baldwin Cemetery, named after the family that owned the property. Arthur D. Baldwin moved his family there from Missouri in 1896, just after the 1893 Cherokee Strip land run. The church was built across from his parcel of land sometime after, and Baldwin offered use of a piece of his property for the cemetery. One newsworthy item for the New Bethany church was in 1942 when it was awarded a $500 bond in a newspaper-sponsored scrap metal drive for the war effort that nearly paid for all **of** their $693 debt. The 40 member church had collected 3,275 pounds of metal. But aside from that tidbit, and the eventual passing of the patrons, there is little known.

Abandoned, the building has become an attractive haven for teens and local cult practitioners. Paranormal teams are attracted to the area for the hotbed of energy that seems to emanate from the old church. While the grounds of the burial site are well-kept, the church is a shell of its former self – crumbling and missing its roof, overgrown with vegetation, and graffiti-laden.

As a point of clarification, I must note that when I have discussed Black Bear church and talked about "occult practices" I have only in **the** sense that there has been some evidence of these things happening *after* the church closed its doors for worship. In no manner have I insinuated that the parishioners of the church practiced in the occult while the church was in use by the local community, although others have spread rumor of that possibility (and I simply stated that others made that claim). The church fell out of use and was abandoned, but while it spent time crumbling there is a location in the back of the church in which animal bones and a scorched spot on a stone slab may likely be a couple of the signs of animal sacrifices and occult practices. The dilapidated state of the building also lends to wild speculation of what has gone on there, and these rumblings turn into local legends that may or may not be true.

Both the cemetery and the church have been deemed as actively haunted locations by many local paranormal teams, including Society of the Haunted. A dark entity known as a **"crawler"** is said to reside within the church while short shadow people lurk outside and peer through the broken windows. The cemetery seems to be inhabited by the ghosts of the local community from long ago.

Also a mystery is the identity of Bartholomew Jenkins. He was introduced to us by a psychic medium who had talent but who was also known to fabricate experiences and readings. We thought she was bullshitting us that night.

EXHIBIT 4
CORRESPONSENSE TO JENKINS

Dear Mr. Jenkins,

You must forgive me that I did not originally believe in your existence. The medium through which you spoke that night has been known to over-exaggerate. That said, I'm still having a hard time believing in the authenticity of your letter.

I have, however, always wondered about the identity of the "Unknown Cowboy" and will begin a preliminary investigation until which time you and I can sit down together and talk about this matter further.

If there is any information about this cowboy that you have been able to put together over the past few years during your interactions with him, please forward that to me. I am, after all, starting from almost nothing here.

Kind Regards,

Mike Ricksecker

EXHIBIT 5
CORRESPONSENSE TO JACK

Dear Jack,

I appreciate you sharing your story with me about your involvement with the cult and the ceremonial work you performed there. You provided some interesting detail that many of us that have investigated the location have long wondered about.

I would love to sit down with you and talk more in detail about your experiences there at the church and the group you were involved with. Given the claims you've made I'll need to authenticate and validate the story as much as I can. I'm sure you understand.

Please let me know what is the best day and time for you. I would appreciate it if we could meet within the next couple weeks.

Best,

Mike Ricksecker

Ghostorian's Note:
My response was returned with invalid email recipient errors.

EXHIBIT 6
REMOTE VIEWER'S IMPRESSIONS

Ghostorian's Notes:

I immediately set out on another follow-up investigation of the Black Bear church and cemetery. Given the last-second coordination of this investigation, no one else from Society of the Haunted was available to go, so I went alone. This is not a recommended practice.

While there, I sent two images to a highly trusted remote viewer, Vanessa – one of the church exterior and one of the stand of trees at the cemetery where shadows are commonly reported to be seen scurrying about and near where we had previously "talked" to Bartholomew Jenkins, just a few paces away from the Unknown Cowboy's grave marker. I was quite surprised by her findings.

Vanessa's Impressions:

I know this may sound bizarre, but the primary figures in both these pics are children. In the building pic I see a little girl running up and down the center of the building. People are gathered there but they can't see her even though I can see her plain as day. She doesn't care because she's free now.

In the cemetery pic I see children peeking around the trees. Almost like hide and seek with each other.

EXHIBIT 7
BLACK BEAR INVESTIGATION

<u>Time of Investigation</u>:
  10:35 PM – 2:47 AM

<u>Arrival</u>:

I parked next to the church as always. There were no signs of coyotes as is sometimes the case at this location, nor were there any teenagers lurking about partying as is also sometimes the case.

I performed and immediate EMF (electromagnetic field) and photo sweep of the church. There were no EMF anomalies at that time and nothing unusual appeared immediately in the photographs.

Out in the middle of nowhere, there is no power here at all.

<u>EVP Session #1, Church, 10:52 PM – 11:28 PM</u>:

This was conducted in the pulpit area where I had captured a photograph of an illuminated ball of light during one of my previous investigations of the location. I discovered nothing of significance during this particular EVP (electronic voice phenomena) session.

One personal observance was the possible shadow movement outside one of the windows, but I was unable to confirm it and it didn't happen again during the EVP session.

Cemetery Sweep:
Like I had done in the church, I conducted an EMF and photo sweep of the cemetery. This also revealed nothing.

EVP Session #2, Cemetery, 11:57 PM – 12:36 AM:
I set up this EVP session at the location in which we had previously interacted with Bartholomew Jenkins, between the Unknown Cowboy's grave marker and the stand of trees. My plan was to personally address each and try to have a conversation with the both of them.

12:08 AM: I thought I audibly heard the word "here" in a male voice and I later confirmed this when I reviewed the audio recording later. There were no follow-ups to my responses.

12:22 AM: In a different male voice than the one from 12:08 AM is the single word, "Brother." I did not hear this audibly. It was only picked up by the audio recorder.

Personal Observations, Church, 12:41 AM – 12:49 AM:
Re-entering the church at this time was a very different experience than when I first entered earlier in the evening. When I crossed the threshold into the sanctuary a chill ran up my spine and my senses were immediately alerted. I snapped a few photographs with my camera but, again, nothing was immediately evident.

A large shadow mass seemed to be lurking near the stairwell to the basement and it slowly dissipated into the depths below. I followed.

EVP Session #3, Church, 12:51 AM – 1:38 AM:

The shadow mass did not appear to be present when I first ventured into the basement. I immediately began recording audio and taking photographs.

12:54 AM: Within minutes of entering the basement and beginning the EVP session the shadow seemed to creep out from the far wall along the ceiling near the back entrance. It circled around the exterior wall and then stopped, seeming to hover in one spot for a while. Again, the shadow slowly dissipated away. One EVP was recorded during this time, a classic, "Get out." I also captured a small illuminated ball of light near one of the windows.

1:07 AM: I explained at a bit of length that I was just curious about who or what he or she was, that I was just interested in learning more about it. In response to the question, "Were you summoned here?" the audio recorder picked up the intelligent response of, "No. I came."

1:12 AM: Audible footsteps near the stairwell were heard, also picked up by the recorder.

1:14 AM: After a few times of requesting, "Come closer so I can properly introduce myself," I felt a heavy breathing near my right ear. The audio recorder did not pick this up and photography captured nothing.

1:38 AM: Concluded session. The activity subsided about as quickly as it had started. I believe the entity left the basement after breathing heavily in my ear. The air about the room seemed lighter and less dense, and all personal experiences had completely ceased.

EVP Session #4, Cemetery, 1:43 AM – 2:47 AM:

1:43 AM: I began another EVP session in the cemetery at the same location. I normally don't do this and switch locations, but given the previous activity and my goal for the evening, I made an exception.

1:56 AM: Again, I heard the word "here" which the audio recorder also captured.

2:02 AM: I spotted shadow movement near the trees and began taking pictures. There was nothing immediately discernable on the camera's preview screen.

2:08 AM: At this time I was asking questions to the Unknown Cowboy about where he was headed when he passed away and I audibly heard the word, "bell." A later review of the audio uncovered another word just before "bell" but it's too muffled to make out. It's a single syllable.

2:12 AM: For the first time all evening the EMF detector finally started being active. Lights on the meter were reaching as high as orange (10 milligauss) and one time reached red (20+ milligauss). For a brief moment near the Unknown Cowboy's grave marker a small blue ball of light danced about. I caught a faint glow of it with my camera.

2:15 AM: I audibly heard footsteps coming toward me from the direction of the cowboy's grave marker. These were also picked up by the audio recorder. What my ears did not hear but was captured on audio was a male voice stating, "Go there." Photographs revealed nothing.

2:22 AM: Activity seemed to have calmed down but I thought I saw a little additional shadow play by the trees again. Photographs revealed nothing.

2:47 AM: Concluded investigation. All is quiet.

Final Investigation Notes:
Again, I find that the two locations have a very different feel to them. The church, once a holy place, is very dark. The cemetery, a place where the dead rest, has a definitively friendlier feel to it.

A review of the photographs revealed two additional notes. One, the photograph of the small illuminated ball of light in the basement of the church seems to have a dark shadow lurking behind it in the window. Secondly, one of the photos of the trees in the cemetery when I thought I saw shadows playing about revealed what may be a small human shadow figures peering out from behind one of the trees, but it's difficult to tell.

All-in-all, it was a fairly active night.

EXHIBIT 8
BLACK BEAR ANALYSIS

Church:

The encounter with the shadow that **lurks** in the basement was likely the famed "crawler" of Black Bear Church. From local legend and the letter that was emailed to me, it is believed that this entity was brought forth to the church by an occult ceremony. However, the response given during the EVP session when asked it if was summoned was seemingly negative, stating, "No. I came."

The illuminated ball of light and the shadow lurking behind it could have been one of the small-statured shadows peering in through the basement window, but that is speculation.

Cemetery:

At the cemetery I caught two distinctly different male voices on audio. I'd like to think that one was Bartholomew Jenkins and the other was the Unknown Cowboy. If so, I'd also like to think that the voice that said "here" twice was Jenkins and the other voice that provided a bit more content was the Unknown Cowboy.

Given that assumption, this cowboy told me "brother," "bell," and "go there." There was another indiscernible word just before "bell" and I'm afraid I am going to have to speculate upon that if I am to go wherever this cowboy would like me to venture to unravel his mystery.

With the church right across the dirt road it seems like the obvious answer might be a reference to a church bell. However, the scant records mention nothing of a bell at the church and the old photographs from investigators more than a decade ago when the roof was still present reveal no location where a church bell may have been placed. It was a small rural church that serviced a handful of farming families. There really wasn't the need for an expensive bell.

It's possible the small dancing blue ball of light near the Unknown Cowboy's grave marker may have been a clue. If the single syllable word that preceded "bell" was "blue" then that could have been a reference to the Blue Belle saloon in Guthrie. That's just the sort of place a cowboy may have been headed to, due south.

I have no speculation at this time regarding the shadows amongst the trees other than they may have been other inhabitants of the cemetery.

EXHIBIT 9
BLUE BELLE BACKGROUND

The Blue Belle Saloon in Guthrie, Oklahoma, had been a hub of frontier activity. Its primary function was as a bar, serving alcoholic spirits to those staking their land claim and more. Established in 1889 under a tent in the same fashion that most businesses were founded in the overnight establishment of the town, the Blue Belle became a staple of Guthrie also serving food and selling cigars. Its popularity was also enhanced by the bordello known as Miss Lizzie's that operated out of the same location. When the permanent structure of the building was finally erected, Miss Lizzie's services were moved upstairs while the saloon continued to operate on the ground floor.

Legends and rumors swirl around the Blue Belle Saloon and Miss Lizzie's Bordello. Outlaws of the old west were frequent patrons, including "Wild Bill" Doolin and his "Wild Bunch" gang, the Dalton Gang, the High Fives Gang, and the Cook Gang. Even the Three Guardsmen, the lawmen trying to hunt down these gangs, which included Heck Thomas, Chris Madsen, and Bill Tilghman, are rumored to have stopped in for the occasional drink.

Miss Lizzie, by all accounts an intelligent church-going woman, exploited the poor and the powerful alike. Families on the brink of losing their homes would sell their young daughters into the service of Miss Lizzie while a catwalk extending to the hotel across the street would provide access to the 17 room bordello for local politicians and affluent visitors. Outlaws and local authority figures are also said to have ventured up the eastside stairwell to the second floor.

One of the more popular ghost stories of the Blue Belle include a young girl that worked for Miss Lizzie named Claudia. Claudia is said to have been sold to Miss Lizzie to save her family's farm from foreclosure, but she was so vocally opposed to the arrangement that her welcome as one of Miss Lizzie's girls soon soured. The local legend is that Claudia was beaten to death and buried within the saloon by the old coal chute which is rumored to be an entrance to the old labyrinth of tunnels under Guthrie. This tunnel was used by prominent patrons of the Blue Belle and bordello that wished to be discreet and would have been a perfect exit for a getaway by whomever may have murdered the girl. Whether or not the murder really happened no one knows for sure, but the spectral cries that emanate from that location have many convinced of her unfortunate demise.

Other sightings include the apparition of the same man frequently seen in an assortment of areas within the saloon, including the bar and around the restroom. Scores of women that have visited the saloon today have felt uneasy in the restroom, and many refuse to use it at all. Another man, angry, with a handlebar mustache and a brown derby hat is said to appear in the basement sometimes and hurl obscenities at those who enter. Additionally, the ghostly figure of a dark haired woman has been seen many times throughout the bar area, and people believe this is the spirit of Miss Lizzie.

EXHIBIT 10
BLUE BELLE WALKTHROUGH

Ghostorian's Notes:

I was unable the secure a full-fledge paranormal investigation of the Blue Belle Saloon, but I was able to coordinate a walkthrough of the premises, including Miss Lizzie's bordello which now serves as a gift shop **above** the bar. For this walk-through I brought along Heather, a sensitive with Society of the Haunted, to see if she could pick up on any of the spirits that have been rumored to haunt the building. She knew nothing of the history of the location upon arrival.

Personally, I enjoyed the tour of the historic location, but there was nothing of significance that stood out to me aside for the possibility of a passing shadow in the basement where there was a heavier palpability in the air than the rest of the building.

As I usually do with most locations, I introduced myself to whatever entities may have been present. I also mentioned the "Unknown Cowboy" to try to illicit a response to no avail.

Sensitive's Notes:

There's a mixture of personalities present which is probably due to all the people that have been in and out of the building over the years. There is definitely a strong female that is present and she commands respect. I don't believe she is evil or means to do anyone any physical harm as long as they don't cross her, but she rules the roost.

There are several male spirits throughout the building, the most prominent one lurking in the basement. He's angry and I sense that he occasionally lashes out with a display of mischief. A couple other men lurk near the bar as if they may have been regular patrons while they were alive and just kept stopping by for a drink in the afterlife.

There's also a sadness about the place as if there has been innocence lost and abuse of children at the location. This seems to be more imprinted upon the building than coming from one specific spirit.

Ghostorian's Analysis:

There is nothing to specifically discern from this walkthrough that would help the case. The history behind the location and the entities that Heather picked up on are interesting, but none of that can be tied into the Unknown Cowboy.

EXHIBIT 10
THE PARCEL

This is an excerpt from my personal case journal...

<u>Day 8</u>:

An unusual parcel arrived today. Wrapped in brown paper with no return address was a pack of vintage playing cards featuring the embossed logo of the Santa Fe Railroad. I'm not sure what to make of that at this point other than the fact that an old Santa Fe train depot stands prominently in Guthrie from which I'd just come, but I always appreciate adding antiques to my collection.

While I was putting the deck of cards on a shelf in the living room, Mary appeared to me in the doorway. Mary is the spirit of a little girl from one of my previous cases who has visited me from time to time. She asked me one question and then evaporated into the air:

"Why are you not trying to find her?"

EXHIBIT 11
CONVERSATION WITH MARY

Every town has its secrets. Every community keeps hidden things that nobody wants to talk about. Shame would scar those that remain, and seldom few ever want to deal with the pain.

Ghostorian's Notes:

The closest large town to Black Bear is Enid, unless you want to count Garber, but there is little more there than a couple gas stations and the co-op. They don't even have a traffic light. Back in the day there was even less. If you couldn't get what you needed in Enid back in the early Twentieth Century, you would make the trek to Guthrie, which had originally been the capital of Oklahoma. This was especially true of any significant business deals, including the sale of people.

Sex trafficking is thousands of years old, was rampant on the Wild Frontier, and America's young girls continue to be exploited as The United States boasts the third largest sex trafficking trade in the world with Super Bowl Sunday being the largest trafficking day of the year world-wide.

<u>EVP Session at home with Mary, 7:43 PM – 8:27 PM</u>:

<u>7:43 PM</u>: I performed this as a "burst" EVP session, asking questions for about two minutes then stopping the recorder and listening back for possible responses. This can generate an almost live type of conversation with a spirit.

My question: "Mary, who do you want me to find?"

Mary: "The girl."

<u>7:47 PM</u>:

My questions: "What girl? Does she have a name?"

Mary: (No response.)

<u>7:51 PM</u>:

My questions: "Mary, what girl do you want me to find? Who should I be looking for?"

Mary: "From the church."

<u>7:55 PM</u>:

My questions: "Which church, Mary? Black Bear Church?"

Mary: (No response.)

<u>7:59 PM</u>:

My questions: "Mary, which church is the girl from? Black Bear Church? Did she go to New Bethany Baptist Church?"

Mary: "Yes. And no."

<u>8:03 PM</u>:

My question: "What do you mean by 'and no'?"

Mary: "She lost her family."

<u>8:07 PM</u>:

My question: "Was she kidnapped?'

Mary: "No."

My question: "Did she get lost?"

Mary: "Yes."

My question: "Did she run away?"

Mary: (No response.)

<u>8:11 PM</u>:

My question: "Where did she get lost, Mary? Around the church?"

Mary: "No. Family lost her."

<u>8:15 PM</u>:

My question: "Where did the family lose her, Mary?"

Mary: (No response.)

<u>8:19 PM</u>:

My question: "Mary, who is this girl and where did the family lose her?"

Mary: "Elizabeth. They went to Guthrie."

<u>8:23 PM</u>:

My question: "Thank you, Mary. Where in Guthrie did they lose Elizabeth?"

Mary: "They needed money."

<u>8:27 PM</u>:

My questions: "Who needed money? The family? Where in Guthrie did Elizabeth get lost?"

Mary: "They lost her because they needed money."

This essentially concluded the EVP session since Mary stopped responding to any further questioning.

EXHIBIT 13
GHOSTORIAN'S JOURNAL

<u>Day 11</u>:

The probable connection between young Elizabeth from Black Bear church, likely the girl Vanessa had seen in her viewing, and Miss Lizzie's Bordello at the Blue Belle Saloon in Guthrie is staring me right in the face. That connection arising again after an attempt to connect the Unknown Cowboy with the Blue Belle is a little more than ironic. But how do these things tie into Bartholomew Jenkins and the mysterious email about the occult practices?

I sifted through all my photographs of the ruined church again trying to see if I had missed anything. Again, the self-illuminated balls of light were unmistakable. There are certainly some sort of spiritual entities that inhabit the place. What I hadn't really looked at before was the graffiti, and I almost missed it while I flipped through.

Back Bear Church has been desecrated time and time again by the local teens who have used the place to party. The walls are littered with spray paint of people's names, crass phrases, and the word "vagina" standing prominent in the dead center of the pulpit wall. There are a smattering of symbols scattered about as well, and I just saw one that I hadn't noticed before and probably wouldn't have if it hadn't been for the parcel I had just received the other day.

Also in the pulpit area was the symbol for the Santa Fe Railway.

EXHIBIT 14
SANTA FE DEPOT

The building itself built in 1903, the Santa Fe Depot in Guthrie is loaded with legends. Some of the highlights are as follows:

While it handled passenger and mail service, and contained a newsstand, railroad offices, employee living quarters, and a Harvey House restaurant, it is also the site in which on December 29, 1910, Governor Charles N. Haskell signed the legislation that moved the capital of Oklahoma from Guthrie to Oklahoma City.

John Fogarty was the conductor of the No. 410 passenger train which was known in its day as "Four Hundred and Fogarty." During the turbulent days of Oklahoma's past with outlaw gangs, boomtowns, and gun-wielding ranch hands, the Four Hundred and Fogarty had the reputation for being the most reliable locomotive on the railway. Tales of Fogarty's toughness, including a few incidents in which pistols were drawn, made the rounds. Nobody got the best of the popular conductor.

There was the great toad incident at the Harvey House when small live toads were found kicking about in the hot coffee that had been served, a mystery until 1953 when an old brakeman of a freight train revealed that he had been the prankster.

In May 1936, a faulty rail just three miles north of the depot caused a horrific train wreck on the bridge over the Cimarron River. One of the railcars plunged 25 feet into the river, killing people aboard and injuring many.

In May 1954, a Santa Fe locomotive halted at Guthrie and remained at a standstill long after it was supposed to have continued on when it was discovered its engineer, John Avery, had died of a heart attack while waiting.

Paranormal activity over the years has included a woman in a long, black Victorian dress is often seen near the second floor dormitory window. Many believe she is the woman who supervised the Harvey Girls as headmistress. Her spirit is seen as the stern and authoritative type, becoming frosty when male visitors venture up to take a peek at where the girls once lived.

Downstairs in the depot area is a bit of residual energy from passengers of long ago that plays back like a recorder and gives the occasional snapshot of the train station from the past with voices and noises coming back to life at seemingly random moments. There may also be an intelligent haunt on the first level as well since employees of the restaurant have found drinks filled on tables and chairs pulled out as like an invitation to sit down.

Also, other paranormal investigators have seen a mist form in the basement and disappear into one of the walls.

EXHIBIT 15
TALE OF THE OLD MAN

Ghostorian's Note:

Upon discovering the symbol I made immediate plans to visit the Santa Fe Depot. I ate lunch in the small diner that is inside the station, but the ladies running the restaurant were reluctant to talk about anything outside the basic history of the building and the movie that was shot there in 2005.

Sitting on a bench outside when I exited was an elderly man in a flannel shirt and tattered trousers who motioned me to him. He stated he had overheard my questions to the waitress and manager, but assured me he had much better answers. The old man allowed me to record him, and below is a transcript of his tale.

"There are a lot of secrets around these parts, son, and most people don't like strangers snooping around, especially if you live outside of Guthrie. Now, don't get me wrong. These are fine folk that live here, real friendly and hospitable-like, but their business is their business and that chip on their shoulder from 1910 is still there for some even if it was back in their grandpappy's day.

Now, it sounds like you got a little girl you're looking for and a cowboy without no name and a church and the old whore house. All you're missing is the man in the derby hat and the lady that done run that house, Miss Lizzie.

Oh, she was a God-fearing woman, straight as an arrow until it came to her profession and whoring out the girls. Somehow that was just fine as long as some of that money found its way back to the church. They even gave the name a nice ring with 'bordello' and made it real discreet-like for the politicians and bankers as if God couldn't see through the walls. And those politicians and bankers, you see, they got the fresh, young ones, the newest girls to Lizzie's stable while the more common folk would get the ladies that had been around awhile, might not even have had a full set of teeth like myself! Ha! But you get what I'm saying, son.

Now there was one girl there that went by the name of Claudia, and by that look I can tell you done heard about her and that she got herself killed. But I reckon you don't really know how she got herself killed. Well, I'm gonna tell you the story, and you can think what you want about it.

You see, Claudia was Lizzie's newest girl, only been around a couple months. Through her righteous church circles Claudia was sold into Lizzie's services from a family in need of money somewhere up near Garber. Of course, Claudia wasn't her real name. The only one that known that, well, that's coming.

There was this man in from Chicago, wearing a brown suit and one of them derby hats. A financier of some sort. He had business here in Guthrie and down in Oklahoma City, but when he was last in out in these parts doing whatever the hell he was doing between Guthrie and Oklahoma City, using the Santa Fe Railway, of course, he was specially requesting the services, for what they call lack of a better term, of Claudia.

Now it just so happens that this here financier had a brother that worked some of the ranches in the area, a sort of outcast from his family who come out here to find a new life on the frontier. Maybe he was runnin' from something back east. Who knows? But this motley cowboy one day walks into his brother's hotel room across the street from Lizzie's and finds him with Claudia. Well, that cowboy tried to scrap with his brother over the girl on account of him taking advantage of one so young, reminded him of their baby sister, he said. So not only did this cowboy want to save Claudia from his brother, but he wanted to save her entirety and all from the whore house and other men.

That cowboy hatched up some plan to go talk to the girl's folks and try to work something out so they could take her back, and in three days' time Claudia would sneak out and ride off with him back to wherever she done come from. But it didn't go too good. No, not too good at all.

You see, there's more behind the story than just some girl getting herself killed over by some coal chute in the Blue Belle. There's always a bigger story, son, and it gets lost to time, so you better listen up to this old codger here before the tale dies with me.

Yeah, Claudia did get herself killed over by that coal chute, but that cowboy was never going to be waiting out there for her. He just didn't know how it all really worked out here, being from back east and all, and he didn't know that dirty family secrets, them skeletons everyone's always talkin' about, need to stay in that closet. Claudia was dead to the family now, you know. She was being defiled by the sin of many men, a sort sacrifice the family done justified to keep the rest of their lives going, so they weren't gonna want to see her no more. Too much shame. Best be forgotten about. And here comes that cowboy riding up to them, may as well been on a white horse, with his promise of bringing the girl back to them.

I reckon it was some kind of surprise to that cowboy when that family refused to take back their own kin. They didn't want no trouble with nobody, but there was gonna be all kinds of trouble with what he was trying to sell. So when he started ridin' off talking 'bout going and getting the girl anyway and they needed to think about what was best for the girl, well, Claudia's old man hit that cowboy over the head with a shovel and killed him. They covered it up by saying that this cowboy fell off his horse, must have had a heart attack or something, and hit his head on a rock. So they buried him up there all real Christian-like as if he's just been some stranger riding through and suddenly died.

Now for Claudia, of course she didn't know none of this, so she was going to make her escape through the old coal chute anyway. That financier, however, caught wind somehow of this plan his brother done hatched up, maybe Claudia told him, and he tried to stop the girl. Until the story became forgotten about some would say he did what he done because he had one of them infatuations with Claudia, and others would say that he was just trying to save his skin because Lizzie known he had a thing for the girl and if she went missing while he was in town, well, Lizzie had plenty of power and connections to make sure he went missing, too.

So, Claudia tried to escape, he tried to stop her, and in the struggle she broke her neck and died. Of course, all that struggling and arguing and fighting was making some sort of racket and Lizzie come downstairs with her shotgun. Once she saw one of her girls dead on the floor she shot that financier point blank in the chest.

The cleanup? Well, it's not all that hard to make some gent from back east disappear out in these parts. They don't know the territory out here and must have gotten mixed up with the wrong crowd, right? The girl was even easier. The bordello girls were regularly roughed up and beaten something fierce by the men that bought them anyway, so it was easy to just say that after so many people done heard the commotion. Now whether or not Claudia is buried by that coal chute like the current legends tell, I don't know.

It's a sad, sad tale, and like you been telling people, Mr. Ghostorian, there are now some sad, sad spirits hanging around the old Blue Belle."

EXHIBIT 16
CORRESPONDENCE TO JENKINS

Dear Mr. Jenkins,

Attached to this letter is the transcript of a conversation with one of the elderly locals in Guthrie, Oklahoma. I think you'll find that the details therein concern your friend the "Unknown Cowboy" that is buried there at Black Bear Cemetery. Perhaps the fact that his story is remembered and will carry on will ease the weight of his soul.

He should also be told that the girl he is concerned about is doing quite well. She is frolicking about the remnants of the church at a younger, more innocent age and is quite happy where she is at. Elizabeth is no longer Claudia and is free.

I believe this satisfies the requirements of what you asked me to investigate. If there is anything else you need, please let me know.

Yours in spirit,

Mike Ricksecker

EXHIBIT 17
THE WARNING LETTER

Dear Mr. Ricksecker,

I know I said I would never get involved again, but they found me and I felt I had no choice. I think your show stirred up some new interest in the church and the group wants to go back and see what else they can set loose. Their intentions are bad, but I can't get out of it. One of the members is a cousin of mine and he said one of "the circle" was doing time, so they need another body. I can't get out of it this time.

I just thought I ought to warn you that they plan to do this. I don't know what all you do during your investigations or if you do any of that protection stuff, but if they raised up that crawler thing before then they might try something even bigger. I don't know.

I'm scared.

I hope you can help.

Sincerely,

"Jack"

EXHIBIT 18
SADUCISMUS TRIUMPHATUS

From: Sect. I

All Histories are full of the exploits of those Instruments of darkness; and the testimony of all ages, not only of the rude and barbarous, but of the most civiliz'd and polish'd World, brings tidings of their strange performances. We have the attestation of thousands of eye and ear-witnesses, and those not of the easily-deceivable vulgar only, but of wise and grave discerners; and that, when no interest could oblige them to agree together in common Lye.

From: Sect. III, II

I say we know so little of the nature of Demons and Spirits, that 'tis no wonder we cannot certainly divine the reason of so strange and action. And yet we may conjecture at some things that may render it less improbable. For some have thought that the Genii (whom both the Platonical and Christian Antiquity thought embodied) are recreated by the reeks and vapours of human blood, and the spirits that proceed from them: Which supposal (if we grant them bodies) is not unlikely, every thing being refresh'd and nourish'd by its like. And that they are not perfectly abstract from all body and matter, besides the reverence we owe to the wisest antiquity, there are several considerable Arguments I could allege to render it probable. Which things supposed, the Devil's sucking the Sorceress is not great wonder, nor difficult to be accounted for. Or perhaps this may be only a diabolical Sacrament and Ceremony to confirm the hellish Covenant.

From: Sect. VIII, VII

And perhaps the Demon himself useth the Imagination of the Witch so qualified for his purpose, even in those actions of mischief which are more properly his; for it is most probable, that Spirits act not upon bodies immediately, and by their naked essence, but by means proportionate, and suitable instruments that they use; upon which account likely 'tis so strictly required, that the Sorceress should believe, that so her imagination might be more at the devotion of the mischievous Agent. And for the same reason also Ceremonies are used in Inchantments viz for the begetting this diabolical faith and heightning the fancy to a degree of strength and vigour sufficient to make it a fit instrument for the design'd performance.

From: Sect. X, IX

But I attempt something more particularly, in order to which I must premise, that the Devil is a name for a Body Politick, in which there are very different Orders and Degrees of Spirits and perhaps in as much variety of place and state, as among our selves; so that 'tis not one and the same person that makes all the compacts with those abused and seduced Souls, but they are divers, and those 'tis like of the meanest and basest quality in the Kingdom of darkness: which being supposed, I offer this account of the probable design of those wicked Agents, viz. That having none to rule or tyrannize over within the circle of their own nature and government, they affect a proud Empire over us (the desire of Dominion and Authority being largely spread through the whole circumference of degenerated nature, especially among those, whose pride was their original transgression) every one of these then desires to get him Vassals and pay him homage, and to be employ'd like Slaves in the services of his Lufts and Appetites; to gratifie which desire, 'tis like enough to be provided and allowed by the constitution of their State and Government, that every wicked spirit shall have those Souls as his property, and particular servants and attendants, whom he can catch in such compacts; as those wild Beasts that we can take in hunting, are by the allowance of the Law our own; and those Slaves that a man hath purchas'd, are his peculiar Goods, and the Vassals of his Will.

EXHIBIT 19
THE BLACK BEAR BODY

Ghostorian's Note:
The link to this blog post was emailed to me, and it appears the report was kept out of the local news.

The Black Bear Body

There are reports from our colleagues in Enid that an unconscious body was found along a dirt road just several yards away from the abandoned Black Bear church and the cemetery across from it. This area has gained popularity in recent years and the caretakers have kept a closer eye on the property. There are even rumors that the ruins of the church will soon be torn down, but that doesn't stop the curious – and others – from venturing inside.

The description of this young man was simply that he was without a shirt and there were several cryptic markings drawn on his back. Was he a part of one of the rumored "ceremonies" that go on there at times or was he just a drunken teen that passed out and was abandoned by his friends? At this point, we don't know for sure. It's a quiet, tight-lipped community that enjoys its privacy, so the locals aren't talking.

In our last investigation there we caught more Class A EVPs from there than we ever had before, including, "He must die!" Our team site has more information, but we believe crawler activity is beginning to increase.

EXHIBIT 20
FINAL THOUGHTS

<u>Day 23</u>:

This has been a mixed case, but I am happy it appears that while solving the riddle of the Unknown Cowboy I simultaneously solved the riddle of "Claudia" at the Blue Belle Saloon, Elizabeth from days gone by at the New Bethany Baptist Church. Perhaps the spirit of the Unknown Cowboy will be more at peace now. It already appears that Elizabeth is blissfully playful around the remnants of the old church.

With that success is also the incomplete case of the crawler that lurks about the grounds. I've only refocused my attention to this issue for less than a month and there is certainly more to be discovered, but more pressing matters are calling my attention, so I will continue to leave this segment open. With the heightened attention around the church at the moment, I'd be a fool to trespass onto the property. I'll send out a few feelers to see if anyone knows any further details about this body that was discovered along the dirt road there and what kind of markings were upon him.

I would also warn anyone else seeking to venture to the property to not do so without express permission from the owners. The cemetery, however, from all accounts I've seen, is public. I expect I'll return in the not too distant future to give my regards to Bartholomew Jenkins, the Unknown Cowboy, the shadows amongst the trees, and the other souls of the deceased that linger there.

Mike Ricksecker
Ghostorian

HORRORS
FROM AN
EMPTY CHAIR

MIKE RICKSECKER'S
GHOSTORIAN CASE FILES

INTRODUCTION

For years now I have been defining the term "Ghostorian" as:

One who researches and investigates a ghost and the place in which it haunts.

I, Mike Ricksecker, am a Ghostorian.

This case returned me to my home state of Ohio and, although I was nowhere near family, it was a case that showed me how far into the abyss a family can fall. I had only just heard of these types of travesties before I took on this case, but in this one I got to see the fallout firsthand.

This began with a simple phone call with an intriguing premise -- a letter that showed up out of nowhere addressed to a child that no one in the family knew had ever existed -- and a mild haunting. I made the trip with Michelle Wu, one of my fellow investigators with Society of the Haunted, as a *preliminary* investigation just to see if it would be worth the while to bring out a full-fledged team with more equipment.

We got quite a bit more than we bargained for.

EXHIBIT 1
A LETTER TO CAROLINE

My Dearest Caroline,

You are far too young yet to understand the contents of this letter, but I pray that in time, perhaps as you near the age of maturity, the words I pen here will give you some clarity. I also pray that your aunt will retain this letter and give it to you at the proper time.

It's with a saddened heart that I rest here, staring out a window down to the yard and street below, waiting for your father to arrive and to be, for the briefest of moments, a real united family. Sometimes I forget his face, and perhaps I should; even my own mother's face is a blur at times. But yours is always so crystalline and pure, rosy cheeks bright and cheerful, eyes of the purest blue.

I feel there is going to be a **breaking** point sometime soon, that you're going to be taken from me like your brother had been. This brief time that I've had with you has been too good to be true, and it's not going to last. They just won't let it.

Please know that I have loved you since before you were born and, no matter what happens, I will always love you. My life over the past few years has been like a fog, memories lucid as if I've watched myself from afar, but one thing is clear. You are my precious angel and I love you with all my heart.

Somewhere in my room I wrote down a few notes while sitting at that window, hiding my recollections from everyone. What I recorded is beyond me at this point, only a shadow of a memory, but perhaps you can find them someday and know the truth of what has happened to us, our little family.

I wish you much love and happiness in your life, Caroline. While it has evaded me I pray that you will be embraced by it.

Your loving mother,

Miriam

EXHIBIT 2
HOMEOWNER'S EXPERIENCES

Ghostorian's Note:

I was asked to use discretion on this case since there is a great matter of privacy that has the family's concern. While they claim there have been overwhelming paranormal manifestations throughout the historic home, they have asked that I keep the investigative team as small as possible. Since this is a preliminary investigation in another state some distance from home, that is quite fine with me.

I was initially contacted by a Mrs. Catherine Lewis who was interested in the historical investigative work that I do in conjunction with the paranormal. The following is what she had told me they'd been experiencing at the house:

"We live in one of the oldest surviving houses in town, still standing after more than 125 years, so to have some sort of paranormal activity going on is really not unexpected. We believe in such things, having extended family in the UK where the knowledge of family spirits in older homes seems to be more readily accepted. We believe our home also has a family spirit, but we want to verify its identity and discover the true story of what happened to her, if it is indeed who we believe it to be.

102 | MIKE RICKSECKER

Activity we've been experiencing includes a chair in one of the second floor bedrooms moving itself near the window. No matter where in the room we place it, the chair always ends up back near the window. We decided at one point to take the chair out of the room and placed it in the adjacent bedroom. We went on a day trip the following morning, and when we returned that evening the chair was returned to its original room near the window. We have let it remain there ever since, although it is disconcerting to walk into the room and find the chair in such an arrangement.

There are unexplained knocking noises that we hear sometimes that seem to come from that room, but we've been unable to find the source. We did notice, however, that on the night we moved the chair out of the room the knocking increased in both volume and frequency, but subsided again after the chair had been moved back.

We also hear the occasional footsteps in the upstairs hallway as well as a strange sort of moan. These are rarer.

Rarer still, downstairs in the study the door has closed on its own and twice we've come to find one of the desk drawers open and the contents disorganized as if someone was looking for something.

Most concerning is the letter we've just discovered on the chair upstairs. We've never seen this letter before and have no idea how it came to be placed on the chair. Also, no one had any idea that Great Aunt **Miriam** once had a daughter named Caroline."

EXHIBIT 3
HOUSE HISTORY

Historic Large Queen Anne farmhouse built in 1876 in Ohio. Due to requested privacy of the family I am not specifying where exactly in Ohio the house is located, and the family name has been changed to protect the innocent (or the guilty, depending on your perspective). The original family to have built the house was the Tyler family who sold the home during the economic depression, which began with a panic in 1893. In January 1894, Finneas Tyler hung himself from the attic rafters. His grieving son, Benjamin Tyler, was a member of Coxey's Army and participated in the first march on Washington, beginning in March 1894, never to return. Presumed dead, it is unknown what happened to him, and the remaining family members sold the house later that year.

The house has been in the hands of the Graham family (Lewis is Catherine's married name) ever since, spanning four generations.

History From Current Owner:

"My great grandparents bought this house in the 1890s and it has been in the family ever since. From my great grandparents the house was passed to my grandfather, my mother, and now me after my mother passed last year. She had only lived in the house for a couple years following the death of my grandparents in successive months.

The concerning part of the house and family history is with my Great Aunt Miriam. Miriam, my grandfather's sister, had a very troubled life and passed away in her early 20s. What is known is that she became pregnant at the age of 16, was sent away to have the baby which was adopted out, and when she returned she fell into a deep depression. She spent her time sitting in a chair in her room and staring out the window to the street and yard below. A local psychiatrist, well known to the family, **was** brought in to speak with her on a regular basis, but when that didn't work she was sent away to a hospital. It was there that she died a couple years later.

EXHIBIT 4
PARANORMAL INVESTIGATION

Preliminary investigation of historic home in xxxx, Ohio.
Homeowner: Catherine Lewis
Time: 8:00 PM - 2:00 AM

Equipment: Given that it's a preliminary investigation, we brought just one small camera kit consisting of four cameras, two of which were placed in the upstairs bedroom, and the other two along the upstairs hall. Personal equipment includes audio recorders, K-Ii meters, Mel meters, digital cameras, flashlight.
We placed the chair in question against the opposite wall from the window.

It was a relatively quiet evening with little activity, but there were a couple key moments:

9:06 PM: Sounds of footsteps in hall... lightly.

9:47 PM: Audible whisper in room. On recorded audio it sound like "maybe" or "baby".

10:52 PM: Downstairs study. Sounded like a drawer had

opened in the desk but none of the drawers had moved at all.

12:06 AM: In the upstairs hallway. During EVP session heard the footsteps again, this time coming toward us but no sight of anyone. Audio recorder caught "need rope".

1:00 AM: Noted that we had been out of the room for two hours and the chair remained exactly as we had placed it.

Approx. 2:15 AM: We had already begun our tear down, wrapping up the video cameras and taking them downstairs. When we ventured back upstairs for a final sweep to ensure we hadn't forgotten anything, we discovered that the chair had been moved to its customary position near the window and a piece of paper had been placed atop. No one had been upstairs and no one had heard a thing move.

EXHIBIT 5
JOURNAL ENTRY #1

Ghostorian's Note:
Found upon the chair in the upstairs bedroom is a handwritten page that appears to be torn out of a journal. At this time we've been unable to locate the journal.

April 27, 1951

I can't believe he's gone. Other girls remarked that I was lucky, that I actually got a chance to hold my baby, even to learn what gender I had birthed. From what I understand this was the result of a new nurse on staff assisting the doctor who didn't know any better, who didn't know that babies were immediately taken away after their cleansing to be given to a wet nurse until later that day when the family arrived to take the child away. The institution didn't want you bonding with the child, an abomination to have one at such a young age and out of wedlock. No one cared to listen to my protestations that Mary, their blessed virgin, was even younger than I when she birthed Jesus and her marriage, at still a younger age than I, had been arranged.

I had met and fallen in love with the most wonderful boy, Johnny Barker. He loved me, and cared for me, and listened to all my dreams and desires until *he* became one of those dreams and desires, so we consummated that love in the moonlight in my bedroom one night last summer when he snuck in through the open window. My brother, nearly eight years his senior, beat him bloody when it was discovered that I was with child. At times I would spy Johnny walking past the house, as did my family on occasion, one of my brothers or even my father scaring him off. He did venture back into my room one time and put his hand over my belly. It wasn't goodbye, he promised. We made love and within a couple days I was sent away until I had our son.

I don't know where my baby is now and I don't know whom he's with. Some of the other girls thought I should give him a name for my own peace of mind, however unlikely his new family would have called him so, while others yet thought that would just bring a greater burden upon my soul. I haven't named him for my own sake. If ever I should meet my son again I should do so if he would allow. It's an opportunity I believe all mothers should have.

Until that day, however, I will continue to long to hold him, his adorable little cheeks puffed out from his swaddling cloth, tiny eyes closed and chest heaving with his first breaths. Perhaps this new family will be ill equipped to handle a baby boy and they will return him to me, if **not** now, perhaps when he enters those fantastically wild years that seem to begin around the age of two. My younger brothers all went through it, frustrating the rest of the household to no immediate end. My heart years for such a gift, for us to be reunited along with Johnny, a true happy family.

I sit here, staring out the window, until that day comes.

EXHIBIT 6
CLIENT INTERVIEW

Ghostorian's Note:

Following the discovery of the journal entry found upon the chair, I scheduled a follow up with Catherine for the following afternoon after a good morning's rest. Originally, I had us scheduled to meet with her again after a full day of rest and evidence review, but given the contents of the letter I wanted to ask a few immediate questions regarding Miriam.

The following is a transcript of Catherine's statements regarding the known history of Miriam:

"My Great Aunt Miriam is a bit of enigma to the current family. Much of her past was secreted away, so we know little. But what I do know is that much of her childhood was much like any other for one who grew up during World War II. Both my great grandfather and grandfather were off to war in the Army for a couple years, but, thankfully, neither saw any real action. Aunt Miriam, along with her brothers, helped my great grandmother collect scrap metal for the war effort. Imagine a bunch of kids running around town scrounging through bins and back alleys for scraps of metal, hounding the local merchants and almost anyone they could find to donate or give what they were going to discard anyway."

Ghostorian: "How many brothers did your Great Aunt Miriam have? Did she have any sisters?"

"There were four brothers that survived. The oldest, my grandfather, was eight years older than Aunt Miriam. There were two boys after him. One was stillborn and the other died of pneumonia at the age of two. After Aunt Miriam there were three more boys.

By all accounts Aunt Miriam was a sweet child, very pleasant and polite, helpful. My grandfather and his brothers would rarely speak of her, but when they did it was with a fondness for her role as an additional caretaker alongside my great grandmother. This business with the boy, Johnny Barker, my grandfather never spoke of, but my Uncle Henry and Uncle William did from time to time, more in the sense that after my grandfather gave Johnny the beating of his life no one dared mess with the family again. But they each expressed a hint of sadness. Apparently, they both rather liked Johnny and thought he was going to eventually become part of the family -- until he got Aunt Miriam pregnant, of course. If they had waited just another couple years or took better precautions then so much would have been different.

But, you know how things went back then. Having a child out of wedlock at the age of sixteen, that was a shame on the entire family, and what happened to Aunt Miriam happened to many other girls back then. She was sent away to have the child, which was immediately given up for adoption and never to be talked about again. She was to return to school upon her return and mask her time away as an illness or some other lame excuse. "

Ghostorian: "What is known for sure when she returned? I'm just getting into the mix now, and given that I've just recently read the letter to Caroline and this journal entry, I'm a little foggy on what was only known before these two items came into play."

"Well, like I told you before, we had no clue about this Caroline or Aunt Miriam possibly having another child. My Great Uncle Henry, who is the youngest of that generation and is the only surviving sibling, is battling Alzheimer's and couldn't possibly answer any questions about it.

What has been passed down over the years and what I know from a couple scant documents is this. After Aunt Miriam returned she fell into a deep depression and confined herself to her room, sitting in a chair and staring out the window for the return of her baby. Apparently, from this new journal entry you found, she was also trying to spot Johnny if he walked by the house. At first, my great grandparents thought the depression would pass, that Miriam would get over it, but she never did. The depression grew deeper and she began eating less and less. At some point they asked a family friend who was a practicing psychiatrist, a Dr. Francis **O'Toole**, to come and see her, which he did on a fairly regular basis for a little more than a year. However, he was unsuccessful in helping Miriam, and after she tried to take her own life he urged the family to commit Miriam, which they did, to Athens State Hospital. Apparently, they couldn't help either since she died about two years later."

Ghostorian: "What was the cause of death?"

"They labeled it as 'Exhaustion From Acute Mania' but I think she just gave up the will to live. The term is really vague and could mean anything, especially considering the type of mental health care back then. It was horrible."

Ghostorian: "Is there anything else you can tell me about Miriam? Any favorites she had as a child? Pastimes? Places she liked to visit? Are any of her belongings still in the house?"

"I really don't know much about that. She played with her younger brothers a lot from what I gather, and she liked to help her mother in the kitchen. She had a knack for breakfast food, apparently. My Great Uncle David used to rave about her French toast. He said no other has been able to make it as she did, and that was all he really ever said about her.

As far as any of her belongings, the furniture in the room is still hers aside from the mattresses and the night stands. The bed, headboard and frame are hers, as are the dresser and mirror and the chair. From what I understand, she originally brought the chair into the room to sit and freshen up in front of the dresser's mirror. I don't know of any smaller personal items that belonged to her that may still be about unless there's something in one of the old trunks in the attic."

Ghostorian: "Interesting. Mind if I look through the trunks?"

"As long as I'm with you, I don't mind. Some of that stuff up there I've never been through."

EXHIBIT 7
GHOSTORIAN'S NOTES

A search of the attics trunks proved fruitless. We found nothing more than a couple trinkets and some old clothing, dresses that may have once belonged to Miriam or, perhaps, even her mother. A music box with a ballerina was found and, although it didn't function, Catherine decided to place the music box on the dresser in Miriam's bedroom. I warned her that the reintroduction of such an item could cause an increase in unwanted paranormal activity, but it seems she's willing to take that chance in order to obtain more answers regarding her great aunt. A journal was not found.

Dr. Francis O'Toole passed away of a heart attack in 1961 at the age of 58. He is buried in the local cemetery next to his wife who passed away in 1973, and it does not appear that he has any family local to the area. Dr. O'Toole worked out of the home and the house no longer stands.

A John Barker resides in the area and, born a year prior to Miriam, seems to be of an appropriate age that he may be the same Johnny Barker the family once knew. I have left messages at the provided phone number to no avail and may pay a visit if the calls are not returned before I need to leave Ohio.

EXHIBIT 8
ATHENS LUNATIC ASYLUM

There are a few places to view the records from the Athens State Hospital, better known as the Athens Lunatic Asylum or The Ridges, including the Ohio State Archives at the Ohio Historical Center in Columbus and the Mahn Center for Archives and Special Collections at Ohio University, and some records are available online. Records regarding specific patients, however, are not available to public, and may only be accessed by the patient, if still living, or the next closest living relative. I've informed Catherine of this and she seems interested in making provisions to acquire the records.

The hospital first opened its doors on January 9, 1874, built of bricks fired from clay dug from the hill atop which the building sits. The main building was constructed to house 572 patients, nearly double the recommended capacity by Dr. Thomas Story Kirkbride's treatise on hospital design *On the Construction, Organization and General Arrangements of Hospitals for the Insane*, upon which Athens was built. The "bat wing" floor plan and Victorian architecture are frequent characteristics of Kirkbride buildings.

Available records indicate that while some of the staff were fully trained, some were not actually trained at all. Employee records also documented the use of hydotherapy, electroshock, lobotomy, and psychotropic drugs on patients. Early records from the hospital indicated some unusual diagnoses as during the first three years of operation 81 men were diagnosed with their insanity being caused by masturbation, the leading diagnosis among patients at that time. For women during that same time period the leading causes of insanity included puerperal condition (postpartum psychosis), change of life, and menstrual derangements.

In December 1978, a patient named Margaret Schilling mysteriously went missing after purportedly playing hide and seek with nurses who became distracted with other duties and forgot to look for her. Her body was discovered over a month later in a disused room by a maintenance worker, reportedly dying from heart failure. An imprint of Margaret's body remained visible on the floor, attributed to the sunlight streaming through the windows and the room being warm enough to facilitate bacterial degradation. "Margaret's Stain" can still be seen to this day and many have claimed to have witnessed paranormal activity in the room.

Renamed "The Ridges" in 1984, the hospital closed its doors in 1993 and is now owned and operated by Ohio University for use as classrooms and office buildings, and the administration building was renovated into The Kennedy Museum of Art.

EXHIBIT 9
JOHN BARKER INTERVIEW

I was pleasantly surprised to receive a phone call from an 81 year old John Barker who was willing to meet with me at his home as long as his daughter was present. I agreed to those terms and went alone. I asked Michelle to follow up with Catherine about setting up a second investigation of the house.

"Let me tell you, Mr. Ricksecker, that this all happened a long, long time ago. I since moved on and married a wonderful woman and together we raised six wonderful children, including my youngest daughter here. Now, I don't want to go stirring up trouble with anyone, and I would rather just leave well enough alone. But since this is the family that is trying to find some answers and not some crack pots from TV, well, I'm willing to offer whatever insight I can, even though Arthur packed me one hell of a wallop years ago."

Ghostorian: "You don't hold any ill-will or resentment about that?"

"Oh, I had it coming, to be sure, especially in that day and age. Sure, I was ready and willing to marry Miriam even though we were so young and she was still in school. I was working for a local bricklayer at the time. I'd picked up a side job with him when I was still in school and continued on for a few years after graduation, so I had some income, however small it was, and figured I was prepared to be husband and father. Ah, the foolhardy youth!

Now, I'll tell you, to this day I'm still unsure about a lot of things that happened. I **only** talked to Miriam the one time after she came home, so after that it was whatever I overheard around town or the little I could squeeze out of her younger brothers.

What she told me is that she'd delivered a son and that very day he was taken away from her. She was happy that she'd been able to hold him for a moment, but completely devastated that he was taken away. You see, she didn't want to give him up, but that's what they did back in those days with teen mothers. It was a public shame to be pregnant at that age, so they sent girls away to hide the truth and when they came back they made up any number of excuses, illness, or what have you. It was absurd since everyone knew. If a teenaged girl was gone for a number of months, you just knew.

Miriam had this fantasy that the baby was going to be returned, that something would happen with the adoptive parents, perhaps they'd grow weary of the work of raising someone else's child, that they would just return him to her. Of course that was ridiculous since the adoptive parents had no way of knowing who the mother was. Even today there are no records to trace. But Miriam -- no, she was going to wait for the boy and wait for me.

She got sick up there in that room waiting, not physically ill mind you, but the solitude started playing funny with her mind. Then they brought in that doctor and, I'll tell you, things started to get worse. The things I heard coming from that house, I just don't understand why they couldn't see it."

Ghostorian: "Couldn't see what? How were things getting worse?"

"Well, again, this is mostly just going off of things I heard. I wasn't able to talk to her at this point. I heard that he had put her on some new kind of fancy medications, some sort of experimental drugs at the time. I have no idea what they were. But I heard that while he insisted they try the medicine with her that she was refusing to eat and was just starting to fall asleep right in the chair. Before that, when she got tired of looking out the window she'd lay down in bed and she would join the family for dinner. But all of that stopped. The doctor, though, wanted time for the medication to take effect and work its 'magic'. Of course that never happened.

Eventually, things got so bad that Miriam tried to kill herself and then they sent her away to the hospital. She died there a couple years later. I don't know how that doctor kept selling them on his treatment plan. Nothing worked, but I guess he was a friend of the family and they trusted him."

Ghostorian: "How did Miriam try to take her own life?"

"Some say she slit her wrists in the bathtub and some say she tried to jump out of that window. I'd believe the latter over the former, but who really knows except the family that was there at the time, and they're all gone."

Ghostorian: "Any word around town about the doctor after Miriam got sent away? Any idea what the relationship with the family was like after that?"

"You know, it wasn't too good, I don't think. It seemed to me it was a bit on the frosty side, but that could just be me making something more out of nothing than what it was since I didn't like that doctor. I didn't see them socializing around town much, but I didn't see them socialize around town much before that anyway."

Ghostorian: "Did you ever hear anything about Miriam having a second child, a daughter named Caroline?"

"What? No. No, I've never heard anything about that. I don't know if that could have been possible since she was in that house staring out the window all the time and then was sent away to the hospital. What did you say the name was?"

Ghostorian: "Caroline."

"No, I've never heard of a Caroline, at least not from that house."

EXHIBIT 10
PARANORMAL INVESTIGATION

Ghostorian's Notes:

I've extended our stay in Ohio for an additional week in order to conduct a full second investigation of the home and to follow up on the current leads regarding Miriam. Since we still only have the equipment that we brought with us this full investigation consists of more time in the home, including some daylight hours. Paranormal activity can happen any time of day; the real only advantage to working at night is the reduced noise pollution. This also gives us additional time to search the home for this mysterious journal and any additional letters.

Full investigation of historic home in xxxx, Ohio.
Homeowner: Catherine Lewis
Time: 6:00 PM - 3:00 AM

Equipment: One small camera kit consisting of four cameras, two of which were placed in the upstairs bedroom, and the other two along the upstairs hall. Personal equipment includes audio recorders, K-II meters, Mel meters, digital cameras, flashlight.

Again, we placed the chair in question against the opposite wall from the window.

6:05 PM: Michelle felt a cold chill cross her path when setting up the cameras in the upstairs bedroom.

6:12 PM: While setting up the cameras in the hallways, footsteps were heard audibly walking down the hall and into the master bedroom.

6:45 PM: Another thorough search of Miriam's bedroom revealed nothing of interest concerning the possible missing journal. Checked for loose floorboards and any possible removable panels in the walls and in the closet. Everything is solid.

6:53 PM: While in the hallway, a faint male voice was picked up on my audio recording saying, "Follow me." Directly following this voice I remark, "Did you see that shadow?" after having seen a faint shadow dart down the hallway.

7:01 PM: **Pursuit** of shadow came up empty.

7:18 PM: While in Miriam's bedroom Michelle caught a faint female voice on audio saying the name "Johnny."

7:26 PM: The chair made a crackling sound as is someone sat down in it. A temperature reading with the mel meter revealed a three degree temperature difference around the chair than in the rest of the room. That's not significant, but worth noting.

7:38 PM: A burst EVP session since the crackling sound of the chair revealed nothing and the colder air around the chair dissipated.

8:00 PM: Decided to change the scenery and moved downstairs into the study.

8:07 PM: A storm began moving into the area. Faint flashes of light and a rumbling of thunder have been heard.

9:00 PM: Absolutely nothing occurred in the study, so we moved back upstairs into Miriam's bedroom.

9:12 PM: During a flash of lightening we visually saw a translucent hand reaching for the chair near the window while a K-II meter that we had placed on the chair spiked into the red. The camera pointed directly at it picked up on a faint outline of the hand that we saw. At that same time we also audibly heard a gravely male yell out, "Whore!" followed by something else that was drowned out by the subsequent thunder. Review of our audio recordings confirmed what we'd heard.

9:21 PM: Catherine rushed upstairs in a panic saying they were hearing a baby crying out in the middle of the yard somewhere during the storm. We ran outside to see what she was frantic about and at first we didn't hear anything while we got soaked scouring the premises for a baby. No baby was found, but at one point we thought we may have heard the cry of a baby upon the air. Given the raging storm it was hard to discern a direction from which it was coming and our audio devices picked up nothing but the pounding rain and thunder.

9:32 PM: Chaos ensued when we returned inside the house. The window in front of the chair in Miriam's room had been flung wide open, drapes were wildly flying about from the wind, and rain was pooling on the floor. We hurried to secure the window and wipe up the mess with towels from the bathroom before the floor was damaged. Catherine was alarmed, but asked us to continue, recognizing that we were making some sort of progress.

9:38 PM: After we had cleaned up and put the room back in order we suddenly recognized that resting on the bed was another torn page from a journal (see next exhibit).

9:45 PM: The entire room had become energized. Our K-II meters kept a steady beat, constantly upticking within the first couple milliGaus indicators while our Mel meters would not fall below 4.0 milliGaus.

9:48 PM: Audible female voice said, "Help me."

9:50 PM: With the high energy in the room at the time we attempted a burst EVP session, asking questions for about two minutes then stopping the recorder and listening back for possible responses with mixed results. This can generate an almost live type of conversation with a spirit.

EVP Session in Miriam's bedroom, 9:50 PM – 10:30 PM:
    9:50 PM:
        My question: "We heard you. Who needs help?"
        Miriam: "Miriam."
    9:54 PM:
        My question: "How can we help you, Miriam?"
        Miriam: (No response.)
    9:58 PM:
        My question: "Can we see the rest of your journal so we can understand?"
        Miriam: "My chair."
    10:02 PM:
        My question: "Where is the journal?"
        Miriam: (No response).
    10:06 PM:

My question: "Are you still sitting in the chair and waiting after all these years?"

Miriam: "My baby."

10:10 PM:

My question: "I'm sorry about your baby, that we was given away. How can we help you?"

Miriam: "No hospital. My baby."

10:14 PM:

My question: "I'm also sorry about you being taken away. How can we bring you peace?"

Miriam: "My head hurts. Then (indiscernible) darkness."

10:18 PM:

My questions: "What happened to your head? Were you hurt? Were you hurt at the hospital?"

Miriam: (No response.)

10:22 PM:

My question: "Were you hurt by the doctor?"

Miriam: "FRANCIS!"

At this outburst the door to the bedroom suddenly slammed shut and all the EMF detectors we had on hand dropped to zero. We tried a few more questions to no avail. The moment had passed us by and we decided to halt the investigation at that point, regroup, and analyze what we encountered.

Ghostorian's Analysis:

This was one of the most interesting nights of my career, extremely active with the haunting of Miriam with, perhaps, a slight overlap of the Finneas Tyler suicide near the beginning. The storm had energized the house and charged the atmosphere for the manifestations of the voices, the cry of the baby upon the air (perhaps), and other activity such as the window flying open. The disembodied hand near the chair coinciding with the exclamation of "whore" seemed

very out of place for the history we'd had at that point, but
the found journal entry would prove to be enlightening.

EXHIBIT 11
JOURNAL ENTRY #2

March 3, 1953

The time is getting near. I can tell. It's similar to the way it was last time, and when I felt this last time baby Johnny was born within the week. Francis wants to hear nothing of it. In fact, he's still insisting that I call him Dr. O'Toole even though he still frequents my bed in order to bond with the baby. I don't know how much longer I can keep this secret. Everyone still thinks that John snuck up into my room last summer, Fran has assured them as much, and now the room that I've secluded myself to has become a sort of prison for me until the baby is born. No one wants Johnny to know, but I seem to be the only one that knows the truth.

I don't think Francis will hold true to his promises. Already he has put off so **many** of the things he said he had in store for us like our own little home in the country for just the three of us, some place away from all the bad memories. He said that's what I needed most, a real chance to get away from everything that has ever hurt me, to get away from the ones that made me abandon my baby. I've been paying retribution for that, but at least God has given me another opportunity for redemption through Francis, a new chance to be a real mother. All I have to do is take my pills and keep the secret until the baby is born and Fran leaves his wife, or maybe it's the other way around. The pills seem to make me a little cloudy on that point, but Francis insists it's not the pills and that they're helping, that he has seen a real improvement in me.

I look out the window now for him, for when he comes to call. Maybe this will be the day he comes to take me away, to fulfill his promises of a beautiful life for us. I was so hesitant at first, when he first called me beautiful, when he first told me how amazing he thinks I am and how I would have made a wonderful mother, when he first touched me. It felt wrong at the time; after all, he was so much older than I and he was my doctor, but he assured me the nervousness was just natural and that being with him would help me with the breakthrough I needed to step out into the world again. He's giving me the opportunity that my parents had ripped away from me two years ago. I just wish he was as sweet as he had been when this all first began.

EXHIBIT 12
GHOSTORIAN'S NOTES

I have double checked the county records for 1953 and there is no record of Miriam having birthed a child named Caroline or otherwise. Catherine also continues to insist that there is no family record of Miriam having birthed a second child, and I have no reason to doubt her. For a fleeting moment the thought crossed my mind that Miriam may have miscarried, but the initial letter that started this case was written from the perspective that the baby was alive. Could that just be a delusion on Miriam's part, a distraught mother writing to the child that never made it alive into this world?

The revelation from the journal entry has us all distressed. This local psychiatrist abused his power and authority over his patient, Miriam, and exploited her for his own sexual gratification to the point that he impregnated her. Just from her brief entry the evidence of grooming and empty promises to coax her into his own selfish desires is blatantly obvious. Given her condition at the time, he likely had the family convinced that the child belonged to Johnny, the result of him sneaking in at night again. After all, who would they believe -- the trusted doctor or the manic depressive who had confined herself to her room for years? There are laws against this now in a number of states as a criminal offense, considered statutory rape in some, but nearly half still need the legislation put into place.

EXHIBIT 13
DOCTOR LOBOTOMY

Catherine discovered additional distressing news about Miriam when looking into her medical records from the old Athens Lunatic Asylum. In November 1953, Miriam Graham, had an invasive medical procedure performed upon her by Dr. Walter Freeman, M.D., otherwise known as Doctor Lobotomy.

Between 1953 and 1957, the notorious Dr. Walter Freeman, a neurologist from George Washington University, performed over 200 frontal lobotomies at Athens State Hospital. Over the course of four decades traveling across the country in his "lobotomobile", Dr. Freeman performed more than 3,400 lobotomy surgeries in 23 different states, about 2,500 of which were of his trans-orbital ice pick variety. This method consisted of inserting a long metal pick between the eyeball and eyelid until it reached the bone at the roof of the eye socket, upon which he pounded the pick through bone and into the frontal lobe of the brain. The same was done on the other side and then he used the picks to sweep through the frontal lobes, severing and destroying them.

It is estimated that up to 15 percent of patients died from the procedure. Many had to be retaught basic functionality such as eating and using the restroom, and relapses into the behavior of which they were supposed to be "cured" often occurred. Nineteen minors were lobotomized by Dr. Freeman, including a four year old. One patient died in 1951 when Doctor Lobotomy stopped mid procedure for a photo opportunity and the pick penetrated too deep into the brain. Freeman was finally banned from the practice in 1967 when Helen Mortensen died of a cerebral hemorrhage following her third lobotomy.

Dr. Freeman's most famous case was that of Rosemary Kennedy, the sister of President John F. Kennedy, who was reportedly prone to violent mood swings, erratic behavior, and was possibly suffering from depression. When she was 23 in 1941, her father heard of a new medical procedure that would help calm her down and placed Rosemary in the care of Freeman and Dr. James Watts for a prefrontal lobotomy, which required drilling two holes into the head. The procedure left the young woman in a near-infantile state, incontinent, often spending time in a blank stare daze, and her speech became an incomprehensible form of babble. Rosemary was institutionalized and took years to learn how to walk again, albeit with a limp. She never regained the use of one of her arms and never spoke clearly again, but was the first of the Kennedy children to die of natural causes at the ripe again of 86 in 2005.

EXHIBIT 14
THE JOURNAL

Ghostorian's Notes:

After Catherine shared with us Miriam's medical records we performed another search of the house for the missing journal. Once again, we began in Miriam's old bedroom and fanned out from there. While in the hallway a loud thud resounded from the attic, but upon looking not a thing was discovered out of place. While in the attic another loud thud was heard, but of a higher pitch, coming from back on the second floor. A quick glance into Miriam's room revealed the source: the chair had been knocked over. I moved to right the chair, but as I did so, the interaction with Miriam through the burst EVP session echoed in my mind:

My question: "Can we see the rest of your journal so we can understand?"
Miriam: "My chair."

Instead of setting the chair upright I flipped it over, and there, strapped to the underside with a slender belt, was an old journal. I gathered Catherine and Michelle and, together, we sat in the dining room and read the final entry together.

June 21, 1953

They're taking me away today. It's as if this is my final punishment for having children, first with the boy that I loved and second with the man that promised to make everything better. Have I done some horrible act in my life that I can't recall that has caused this curse to be placed upon me? I would have loved my children, but they were both stolen from me far too soon. I just wanted the opportunity to really mother the children I bore, but now my grief over them has become their cause to send me away to some hospital. That's Fran's recommendation, of course, to cure my "wild mood swings".

Why does nobody understand? I've been grieving for the loss of my son and, finally, when I have an opportunity to raise a daughter her life is extinguished before it really even had a chance to begin. They say she just died in her sleep, that it happens with babies sometimes and there's no reason for it, but I know he did it. I know Francis murdered my baby Caroline. Perhaps he snuck into the room at night while I was sleeping, the way Johnny used to. I don't know, but he couldn't stand it when I referred to her as "our baby." It would anger him and he would slap me for it, but then I started getting angry back.

I don't understand why, but my parents always took his side; they always believed him over their own daughter who was really just silently screaming for help. When I finally screamed out loud they took it for me being crazy. I'm not crazy, but that's what they believe, and Francis has only enforced that belief, has nurtured it like I would have nurtured my children. Whoever says that a psychiatrist doesn't have any power is completely naive. My life was placed in his hands, trusted to help me through a difficult time while I grieved the loss of my son, and now my life is completely destroyed.

I don't know what will come of me at that hospital, but I doubt I will ever see my home again. I doubt I will ever be able to visit the tiny little grave of Caroline again, and I know I will never get the opportunity to meet my son, no matter how much I wished for it over the years. I cannot take anything with me, so I will hide these memories in the one place my parents or Francis will never look. They will try to expunge any memory of what really happened here like they did with my children, but I won't let that happen. One day, the truth will finally be known.

I can only hope that I will be alive to see that day.

EXHIBIT 15
CAROLINE

Two weeks after Michelle and I left Ohio the body of Caroline Graham was discovered and exhumed from the old flower garden at the back of the lot of the historic home. It is believed that the garden dates to the time that the child would have died and was put in place to conceal her grave, along with any knowledge of her existence.

Unofficial estimates determined from the remains of the child place her age at about two months, but with no records of her birth it is difficult to surmise an exact age. Officially, her age is "infant".

The family plans to give the baby a proper burial with her mother who was buried near her own parents at the local cemetery. My personal opinion would be to also exhume Miriam and intern her along with the baby as far from her parents as possible. Francis O'Toole was a monster, but her obtuse parents set up Miriam's life on a path that only ended in destruction.

EXHIBIT 16
FINAL THOUGHTS

This was an emotionally challenging case, one in which it's been difficult to reconcile a sense of accomplishment through the heartache. On one hand, we were able to uncover the secrets the family had been seeking and we picked up some phenomenal paranormal activity along the way. However, the outcome of Miriam's life was absolutely horrific. First, her child was taken away from her, then she fell into a deep depression, the doctor that was called in to help her abused, exploited, and **raped** her, her second child was murdered, she was sent away to a lunatic asylum where they performed a lobotomy on her, and there she died young. Whatever promising life she may have had was extinguished at the tender age of 20.

It's my hope that the spirit of Miriam Graham will be at peace now that her story has been made known and her child has been reunited with her. The truth was hidden for far too long.

Remaining at the house is, I believe, the spirit of Finneas Tyler. The family doesn't seem to be eager to follow up on his small haunting and seem to be content with his periodic footsteps and whispers. Perhaps it will be a case for another day.

INTRODUCTION

For years now I have been defining the term "Ghostorian" as:

One who researches and investigates a ghost and the place in which it haunts.

I, Mike Ricksecker, am a Ghostorian.

I don't claim to be a psychic whatsoever. I've worked with a number of people in the paranormal field that have gifts that I could never fully comprehend. I've witnessed people accurately predict the future, have intelligent conversations with spirits, track down dead bodies, and described rooms in detail while being thousands of miles away under the terms medium, clairvoyant, sensitive, and the like. Many of the good ones will tell you that it is both a blessing and a curse.

If I possess any sort of "super power", for lack of a better term, and people have told me that I am more sensitive than I give myself credit for, it is with my dreams. There have been scores of incidents in which a dream of mine has come to pass, and I am left standing there in awe. The problem in using my dreams as any sort of tool is that not all of my dreams come true and I never know how long it will be until something I've seen ends up happening. Sometimes a vision that I had in a dream may occur in real life within the next couple days, perhaps even weeks, and I've even see them come to pass years down the road.

This Ghostorian Case File is from the folder in my file cabinet marked "Dreams." It is not all-inclusive since many of the dreams that I've had that have come true are very private in nature, but this should give you enough of a sampling to understand what I'm talking about.

EXHIBIT 1
MONTPELIER MANSION

When I first agreed to write *Ghosts Of Maryland* I had a dream that I was investigating a haunted house and felt a strange presence near me when I sat down in a chair in a large front hall. After a time I tried to stand up, but the presence kept pushing me back down onto the seat. Finally, whatever the force had been gave way and I was able to rise, but it then shoved me toward the front door. My dream self got out of there as quickly as I could.

When I arrived at Montpelier Mansion to research the building for my book I discovered the grand front hall from my dream greatly resembled the central passageway in the mansion and that sense of déjà vu encompassed me. I did not, however, attempt to sit on any of the furniture while I was there.

EXHIBIT 2
THE JUNGLE

It was October 1992, on leave between my time in Air Force tech school and my first duty station at Elmendorf AFB, Alaska, and I was sitting in Burger King with my friend, Kelly. We were chatting away about all kinds of different topics, including spirituality and religion. Somewhere in the midst of that conversation I told her about one of the most unusual dreams I'd had up to that point, but I'd had it when I was a small child.

I was in a jungle in the middle of a war zone, presumably one the soldiers in the conflict. While I was firing away with whatever gun I'd been holding an enemy soldier appeared right in front of me, put a pistol to my forehead, and pulled the trigger, shooting me at point-blank range. Immediately, my **vision** became a mix of vibrant colors. Reds, blues, greens, and yellows swirled about like some sort of psychedelic acid trip although, of course, I'd never had one of those before. After a few moments the colors faded away and I was back in the jungle, however, I was completely alone. The battle had stopped and all was deathly still and quiet. In fact, it appeared as if the battle had never occurred or, at least, was far past over and everyone had left, taking the dead with them. It's also possible that I was someplace else in the jungle that looked similar to the location in which the battle had taken place. I couldn't be sure, but one thing that I distinctly felt was that I had died in that dream.

Among the folklore that we pass along to each other as children is that you dream in black and white and if you die in your dream you die in real life. Neither are true. The colors in my dream had been extremely vivid and I had most certainly died. You don't survive that kind of gunshot. What became the question as I got older was, "Had the dream been a vision of a past life? Was it how that life had perished?"

Immediately, the thought of Vietnam springs to mind. I was born in 1974, after all.

Kelly was certainly interested, but what followed my description to her was completely unexpected. A man that had been seated near us rose from his table and handed me his phone number, explaining, "I don't usually do this, but I couldn't help overhearing your conversation about your dream. I'd love to talk to you about it sometime."

He abruptly left, and I never did call him. I was still young at the time and a bit uneasy about the idea of a complete stranger wanting to talk to me about my dreams. Now I wish I'd called.

EXHIBIT 3
MANSION INVESTIGATION

It was a **historic** Victorian home looming before us as we pulled into the driveway. A few of us stepped out of the vehicle, although I don't recall all of who was in this group at the time. Moments later I was ascending the sweeping front staircase up to the second floor, and I looked down into the main entrance hall of the house. My eyes spotted floating apparitions of spirits from years gone by, but this seemed normal to my dream self.

I ventured down the long hallway to the back of the house where there rested a smaller staircase that led to the kitchen. I descended the staircase, and in the kitchen stood one of my teammates from the paranormal team that would become Society of the Haunted. We spoke a little of the activity that I had spotted, and I stepped back toward the rear entrance of the house where a couple dogs were yapping outside.

End of dream.

About a year later, a real life paranormal investigation took me to the house from my dream. Both staircases were there, including the one that led into the kitchen, the railing I looked over when I spotted the apparitions in my dreams, and the dogs yapping in the backyard beyond the rear entrance from the kitchen.

We captured some mild activity that night, but my paranormal experience with that house had already happened a year earlier in my sleep.

EXHIBIT 4
SKELETON IN THE CLOSET

It was in the closet. I knew it was in the closet although I couldn't see it. I opened the door and looked down next to the shoe rack. There in the empty space I knew it was trying to hide. *Skeletons in the closet.*

I reached down with both hands, grabbed at the air, and caught it. I yanked the invisible being out of the closet and carried it into the bedroom. I wasn't sure exactly what I was going to do with this thing except I knew I wanted it out of my house. Suddenly, the entire room started shaking, objects on the nightstand and headboard of the bed toppled over, and a searing electricity scorched my hands. It was fighting back and trying to get loose, but I held tight.

With all my might I reached back and thrust the entity up toward the roof. At the top of my lungs I yelled, "Get out!" and woke straight up in bed.

EXHIBIT 5
ROCKY BALBOA

I have never met Sylvester Stallone, but for a time it seemed we shared some sort of odd connection on one subject only -- *Rocky* movie plot ideas. I've loved the *Rocky* movies as far back as I can remember first ever viewing them, sometime just after *Rocky II* came out. This was in my very early childhood, but I've been akin to writing ever since I understood how to start expressing some sort of thought through words on paper. At my grandparents' house in Ohio the summer I turned seven years old (1981), after having attempted to read one of the *Rocky* novelizations on the long drive to their house from where we lived in Massachusetts, I wrote my own version of *Rocky III* which didn't come out in theaters until the following summer. In my story Rocky Balboa and Apollo Creed became friends and Rocky fought a Russian boxer.

Yes, that's right.

Out of thin air I tabbed two major plot lines for each of the next two *Rocky* movies. Rocky became friends with Apollo in *Rocky III* and he fought a Russian boxer in *Rocky IV*. But I'm not done.

During a conversation with my mother following *Rocky IV*, I made the comment that I missed seeing Rocky as a regular guy without any money like in the first two movies, that it would be nice if he could somehow go back to that should there ever be a *Rocky V*. Voila! A few years later *Rocky V* came out and Rocky lost all of his money finding himself back in the old neighborhood. Unfortunately, the fifth movie in the series wasn't very good and the franchise went into hibernation for a long time.

Then there was the **dream**. Sometime around the turn of the millennium I had a dream that a *Rocky 6* was finally made, and within the dream I was actually watching it. The scene I observed was a deathbed scene in which Rocky's wife, Adrian, was dying. It was rather heartbreaking, and I actually woke up with tears in my eyes. Fast forward to 2006 when the movie *Rocky Balboa* was the surprise movie hit of the holiday season -- and the movie started with Adrian deceased, bringing us to tears with old memories and Rocky's pain (as well as Paulie's).

I can't say there has been any connection with the new *Creed* movie, technically the seventh in the franchise, although Stallone is on record saying that the new movie is *Creed 1* and not *Rocky 7*. Sly didn't write the script, so that may be, perhaps, why nothing entered my mind about this new spin-off into the *Rocky* universe. But for those four other movies, there was certainly some sort of connection.

EXHIBIT 6
THE FLAME

The incident with the flame wasn't a dream, but I certainly entered some sort of lucid **state**, so I believe it may be somewhat related.

I was raised Catholic and have always felt a strong sense of spirituality throughout my entire life. During high school I was going through my confirmation classes and one of these required attending a mass one weekday evening. I do not recall the purpose of this particular mass, but I remember what happened that night.

While the priest was conducting the monologue of his homily I began staring at a candle near the baptismal. Without realizing what I was doing I began putting myself into a trance and did something that absolutely shocked me.

With my eyes fixed on the flame, words formulated in my mind, "Higher. Higher!"

Sure enough, the flame rose higher and continued to rise at least a foot into the air as my mind repeated the words. I have no idea if anyone noticed, it was a rather small crowd, after all, but once it occurred to me what was happening, my utter shock and surprise broke the trance and the flame returned to normal. I couldn't believe what I'd just done. I had willed the flame of the candle to burn higher!

I briefly tried to do it again, but my nerves were shot from the experience and my adrenaline was rushing, so I was unable to return to the **trance**-like state.

As of this writing, I have yet to attempt this again as an adult.

EXHIBIT 7
THE FLIGHT

I swooped down out of the sky as the battle raged on below. Smoke filled the air, but it didn't distress my lungs as I flew toward the house. My body felt light and quick, and I moved with a purpose. The house quickly rising toward me was my goal. I passed through the roof and ceiling with ease and landed in the middle of a small bedroom.

In the closet cowered a mother and her child. I beckoned for them to come with me. The woman covered the child with her body, pressing the small being hard against her as she shook her head, "No."

I pleaded with her and reassured her that everything was going to be all right, that the blasts echoing from **outside** wouldn't hurt them if they came with me, but they had to leave with me right then and there.

She still refused and familiar words from scripture about people hiding in caves entered my mind. I shook my head and flew back out of the house, saddened.

EXHIBIT 8
THE FINAL BATTLE

The auditorium was packed with a church congregation listening to the character on stage bellow forth with some sermon. I say he was a character because I immediately related him to a televangelist promising to save everyone's soul for a quick donation into his bank account. I stood in the back of the auditorium near the doors and shook my head. Someone I couldn't see outside the doors told me to come along, that I didn't want to be around those people because of what was about to happen.

A few years later in real life I did become involved with such a church with televangelist-type speakers, and they met in a high school auditorium on Sundays that was the exact same one from my dream. It took far too long for me to put the pieces together, but I did finally leave.

Back in the dream world I was lifted in to the **sky** near my old neighborhood from when I was a kid in Massachusetts. Explosions and fires rang out and the ground shook below me. Beings were in the air fighting with each other, and the one before me was ugly and grotesque, much like a Minotaur, but blood red with smoke emanating from its pores.

We flew toward each other and clashed, neither of us getting the better of each other. We clashed again with the same result, shouts and angry grunts ringing out. We stared at each other and I called out, "You're just angry that after this is over you're not going to exist anymore!"

We charged each other in the air again and clashed together once more. This time I smote my opponent and he fell, defeated. I floated for a moment more, satisfied.

I looked about and the skies began to clear. I eased back to the ground where everything was suddenly peaceful and beautiful. Birds chirped and butterflies danced about us. There were several of us walking down the street of my old neighborhood remarking about the vibrant colors, the fresh air, and the peace that now existed.

FRIENDS
OF
THE
FEDORA

This **communiqué** was received from the one that has identified himself as "The Unforgiven One" in this puzzling case taken on by private investigator Chase Michael DeBarlo. For those not acquainted with this case, please refer to the following:

http://www.mikericksecker.com/secret.html

You have heard me, but you have not listened.
These things are of the opera of my life.
Few understand.
Fritz versteht.
Ah, Fritz. Ein Kämpfer für ihr liebst.

Man out of time.
Man misguided.
Man stumbling down the broken road.
A boulevard of broken dreams with few avenues still available.
Which direction at the next fork?

The sun still rises.
Rays of light twist their thin tendrils through gnarled branches.
The brambles thicken.
Leaves darken and grow brittle at dusk.
Are these my same hands?

There they stand beyond the borders.
Blind am I to the path.
Spun about to make an aimless try, but try I must.
There is no other option.
Redemptive road is rendered.

Journey as jagged as my musings.
Is that a mane on top of his head?
Do you remember who you were?
Do you remember what you are?
Truth is strangled by the thickening forest.

Caught in the depths is the truth.
After five all is told.
Can they work it out?
Can they find the secret that hides within?

Count the lessons you have learned.
A tale's moral is many-layered.
Cracks may be found in the sanded lot.
Chasm's wide, but not for Benny.

Can the road be shortened through the wood?
After daybreak we can make our move; I'll go first.
Cynical minds may not forgive.
Can you take that first step if I step, too?

Clear my record.
Altered last reality.
Clear my record.
Clear my record.

What do you think, my dear Mr. DeBarlo? Can not your cohort, Rock Rickman, famed computer genius that he is, crack the code? Didn't you both want to be detectives, or do you just play ones in dime novels?

I am not bashful enough to feign that I am taunting you. Of course I am taunting you, and I am freely willing to boast that I am besting you in this little game. What humors me is that you know the secret and you have repeatedly failed to unlock it.

I'm on that path, DeBarlo. Come join me on it. Meet me half way and we can walk the rest of the way together to where we both need to go -- and bring that damned Rickman with you if he's willing to venture out of his little cave. If not, I will just linger outside your office and prey upon your weaknesses and insecurities. Don't pretend they don't exist; that would make you ordinary.

The road doesn't just go ever on, it's eternal. Start the journey and stop pussyfooting around! Watching you fumble through this just makes me want to explode with more unforgivable acts.

Remember Sammy Jankis? Sammy was a faker. There is more to the truth, so much more good than bad if the Eskimo would just get past his anger and remember. But Sammy has him conned. You know of whom I speak. He may be the furthest down the road, but on the road he is. They all are.

Eskimo, Lynnski, Bubala, and The Man. That's the bigger mystery, DeBarlo, not I. I am but a means to get there, of sorts. While I am a threat to you, you need me -- at least for a time. I'll find my own way once our journey together is complete. Our fates are separate, but we must travel the same road together for a while. I've been lurking, waiting for you to emerge.

Come to me.

ABOUT THE AUTHOR

Mike Ricksecker is the author of the historic paranormal books *Ghosts of Maryland*, *Ghosts and Legends of Oklahoma*, and *Campfire Tales: Midwest*. He has appeared on multiple television shows and programs as a paranormal historian, including Animal Planet's *The Haunted* and Bio Channel's *My Ghost Story*, Fox 5 News (Washington DC) and Fox 25 News (Oklahoma City), and he produces his own Internet shows *Ghosts and Legends* and *Paranormal Roads*.

Mike's historic paranormal articles have been published in *The Baltimore Sun* and *Paranormal Underground Magazine*, and his work has been featured in *The Oklahoman*, *The Frederick News Post*, Marshall University's *The Parthenon*, and Louisiana State University's *Civil War Book Review*.

Additionally, Mike is an Amazon best-selling mystery author with two entries to his Chase Michael DeBarlo private detective series, *Deadly Heirs* and *System of the Dead*.

Mike is a father of four, an avid baseball fan, and a paranormal investigator and "Ghostorian" with Society of the Haunted.

Other titles from Haunted Road Media in which Mike Ricksecker has appeared:

Almost everyone has a ghost story. Real people. Real stories.

Read about haunted houses and vehicles, experiences during paranormal investigations, visits from relatives that have passed on, pets reacting to the paranormal, psychic experiences, and conversations with full-bodied apparitions.

ENCOUNTERS WITH THE PARANORMAL reveals personal stories of the supernatural, exploring the realm beyond the veil through the eyes of a colorful cast of contributors.

The definitive vision of the first Chase Michael DeBarlo mystery novel!

Extended scenes! Foreword from the author! Tons of extras added in an appendix, including DeBarlo short stories published for the first time EVER!

Read Chase Michael DeBarlo like you never have before!Saying Earl Kiddering is rich is like saying Babe Ruth hit a couple of homeruns, but saying he's dead is more accurate. A month after the billionaire drowns in his own swimming pool, Earl's great-niece, Genelle Starr, hires private investigator, Chase Michael DeBarlo, to find Kiddering's missing will while other family members squabble over the fortune.

Deadly Heirs delves into the loyalties (and disloyalties) of family bonds, exposes a private investigator's time management crisis that could endanger human life if not handled correctly, and uncovers the corruption of a mysterious art market.

For more information visit:
www.hauntedroadmedia.com
and
www.mikericksecker.com

Photo by Alison Paylor, 2015

www.ingramcontent.com/pod-product-compliance
Lightning Source LLC
Chambersburg PA
CBHW070552180626
46817CB00005B/1801